GREEN BOY

SUSAN COOPER

GREEN BOY

MARGARET K. McELDERRY BOOKS

NEW YORK – LONDON – TORONTO – SYDNEY – NEW DELHI

MARGARET K. McELDERRY BOOKS

An imprint of Simon & Schuster Children's Publishing Division

1230 Avenue of the Americas, New York, New York 10020

For information about special discounts for bulk purchases, please contact Simon & Schuster Special Sales at 1-866-506-1949 or business@simonandschuster.com.

The Simon & Schuster Speakers Bureau can bring authors to your live event. For more information or to book an event, contact the Simon & Schuster Speakers Bureau at 1-866-248-3049 or visit our website at www.simonspeakers.com.

Also available in a Margaret K. McElderry Books hardcover edition

The text for this book is set in Goudy Old Style.

Manufactured in the United States of America

0713 OFF

This McElderry paperback edition published August 2013

2 4 6 8 10 9 7 5 3 1

The Library of Congress has cataloged the hardcover edition as follows:

Cooper, Susan, 1935–

Green boy / by Susan Cooper.—1st ed.

p. cm.

Summary: Twelve-year-old Trey and seven-year-old Lou, who does not speak, cross the barrier between two worlds, that of their island in the Bahamas, and a land called Pangaia, and play a mysterious role in restoring the natural environment in both places.

[1. Environmental protection—Fiction. 2. Brothers—Fiction. 3. Mutism—Fiction. 4. Lucaya (Bahamas)—Fiction. 5. Bahamas—Fiction. 6. Science fiction.] I. Title.

ISBN 978-1-4424-8081-0 (hardcover)

PZ7.C7878 Gp 2002

[Fic]—dc21   2001030954

ISBN 978-1-4424-8082-7 (paperback)

ISBN 978-1-4424-4122-4 (eBook)

For Chris and Jenny Kettel
Basil and Jane Minns
true islanders

This we know:
The earth does not belong to us
We belong to the earth.

—CHIEF SEATTLE, 1854
in the film *Home* by Ted Perry

GREEN BOY

ONE

It was a little fluttering sound in the roof, moving. The living room of Grand's house reaches up high, with beams across it, and one side open to the porch. Along the top beam the little sound ran, very soft, you could scarce hear it. Then at the wall it turned, and came fluttering down a side beam. You could begin to see a shape now. So small: was it a moth? A spider?

Lou was watching. He moved toward it.

"Careful," I said. "Don't touch. Might be poisonous."

The little fluttering thing slid down to the floor and rested there. I saw a tiny foot. It was a bird.

Lou crouched down beside it and put out his hand. Somehow he knew how to rest his finger behind the bird's feet so it stepped onto his hand. Then you could see clear: it was a tiny hummingbird, and it was all wound around with sticky spider-silk, so that it couldn't fly, nor hardly walk. It must have blundered into a powerful big spider's web. Now it was all trussed up, terrified, there on the palm of Lou's hand.

Lou made a little comforting sound at the back of his throat. Slowly and very carefully, with his other hand, he pulled the fine sticky strands away from the bird's legs and wings. His fingers were so small and gentle; after all, he's only seven years old. The bird didn't move.

There it stood on his palm, bright green, an emerald hummingbird. It was the most beautiful thing I've ever seen. Its throat was red, and its feathers all different shades of green, gleaming. The spider-silk was all gone now, but still the bird didn't move. It must have been totally exhausted.

Lou gazed and gazed at the bird, and the bird looked back at Lou.

"Take it outside," I whispered. We moved out of the room, across the porch, to the hibiscus hedge, all starred with yellow-centered red flowers like trumpets. Hummingbirds love hibiscus. But the tiny bird still rested there on Lou's hand, not moving; as though it was giving Lou a present, staying so that he could look.

It was so beautiful, I can't tell you.

At last it flew, and hovered beside a flower, and darted away.

"Oh man," I said. I couldn't think of anything else to say, it was so amazing.

Lou smiled at me, and made his happy sound, that's as close as he can get to a laugh.

My brother Lou doesn't talk, and he has a few other

problems too. He's different. But I'm used to it. My name is Trey, and I'm a writer. I look after him. I'm twelve years old. This is my book, the story of what happened to Lou and me.

TWO

It was the next day, and we were out in our boat, heading for Long Pond Cay. There was a small breeze, but the water was way calm, and the tide coming in. The boat is a battered nine-foot dinghy that Grand let me have when I came ten years old, though it wasn't the birthday that did it, it was my growing enough so that my head touched the five-foot mark on the wall. That mark had been there through all my uncles growing up, and my mother and my aunts. Grand said you had to be that tall to have the strength and size to row a boat.

The boat's pretty old. It was the runabout for one of the American sailboats that come here for the winter. The American's wife had given him a new dinghy for a Christmas present, so he asked Grand to get rid of the old one. Get rid of it? No way! Grand and I re-fiberglassed it. You'd have trouble sinking that boat now even if you tried.

When I came eleven and I rowed well enough to get across to Long Pond Cay and back, Grand let me have a little fifteen-horse outboard motor. He taught me to take it apart and put it together again before he'd let me use it, and though it's even older than the boat, I can fix it when it goes wrong.

So sometimes they let me take Lou out in the boat, for the whole day if there's no school. Grand and Grammie have been raising us for as long as I remember, because our father went away long ago, and our mother has to work in Nassau. They're old, Grand and Grammie, but they're busy too; she works in the bank in town, and he runs his bonefishing school, teaching tourists how to catch the quick glittery silver bonefish that feed on the flats all along our side of the island, or sending them out fishing with guides. He's got eight boats, flat quiet boats with little motors not much bigger than mine, and six guides. He has a little farm too, where we grow bananas and papayas, tomatoes and squash and onions. He's busy. So he trusts me to keep Lou busy, when there's no school.

There was no school this day. It was June. We puttered along the broad channel between our island and Long Pond Cay, with the sky clear blue overhead, and the water that chalky light turquoise-green that comes from the sunlight bouncing up off the white sand under the sea. There's shallow water there always, not deep even at high tide, and the banks of sand under the water shift all the time, never the same from one year to the next. But I know where they are, always, Grand and me, and the bonefish guides.

Lou stood up in the bow, looking out for his favorite birds. He gave a little pat on the gunwale, to catch my attention, and pointed up—and there was the osprey, the big fish hawk, high up, coasting, the light from the water sending up a greenish tint to the underside of his broad white wings. He called down: *peeeu, peeeu,* a little high-pitched sound that always sounds undignified coming from such a great grand bird.

I knew he was calling to his mate, but it sounded for all the world as if he were calling to Lou.

I swung wide round a sandbank still mounded white out of the water; the tide was coming in, but it wasn't halfway yet. Nobody comes down this channel but Lou and me; the guides go a different way to get to the bone-fish flats, and the water is too shallow for the tourists' sailboats—they're afraid of going aground. This is our place.

"I'm going ashore by the tree," I said to Lou. "Throw out the anchor when I say."

He got down and made sure the bow anchor wasn't tangled in its line, and I saw him look to make sure the other end of the line was tied fast to the boat. He's a good little crew. Then I headed for the beach in front of the biggest casuarina tree at this end of the island; we use it as a landmark because it's so tall. You could hear the wind whining through the needles on its feathery branches. Grand doesn't like casuarina pines, he says they're invaders from Australia and they drive out the native trees. But I like the way those feathery branches reach up in all directions, and the spooky way they make the wind sing.

"Now!" I called to Lou, and he tossed the bow anchor out. When the line had run out after it, I killed the motor and Lou came hopping back past me for the other anchor in the stern. That's Grand's rule: off a sandy shore, the boat must be moored at both ends. I tilted up the motor to keep the propeller out of the sand, and Lou jumped out and splashed ashore carrying the stern anchor. It's a light anchor but that's hard work for him, he's not very big. He loves doing it.

He marched up the sand as far as the line would let him go, and dug the anchor in.

"Good!" I called. Now the boat would stay there, held between the two lines, while the water rose with the tide.

I splashed out after him with my backpack, and we walked where we always walk at first, along the broad white beach that curves for a mile or more around a great peaceful bay, where the sea is always shallow and quiet except in a storm. We were both keeping an eye out for sunrise tellins, Grammie's favorite shells, double ovals tinged with yellow and pink, but there weren't any today. I could see three rows of footprints, made by large adult sneakers. Some early walkers had been there before us.

Lou ran ahead of me. Partway down the beach, he

turned away from the sea, into the grass and scrubby bushes that went up from the sand, scattered with casuarina trees trying to find a place where they could grow tall. They were out of luck here; on this part of the beach, a few years back, the waves from a huge storm had eaten away the sand to expose the rock. It wasn't really hard rock, but a kind of whitish sandstone, made of layers of sand squished together for hundreds of years by their own weight.

The rock was cut away like a little cliff, and you could see the thin, thin layer of soil on top, and the skinny black roots of the casuarina trees dangling, reaching out from trees twenty feet away. When the soil's that thin, I guess the trees have to send their roots a long way out to find a place to live.

Lou disappeared. He'd found the gap in the rock that we called our cave, though it wasn't much more than an opening, and only kids could have got inside it.

"Hoo, hoo!" I heard his monkey sound, that's just like the sound I remember from a movie on television about chimpanzees.

"Hoo! Hoo!" He was out on the sand again, jumping about, agitated, beckoning me.

"What's up, Lou?"

I went up to the cave. It's only about ten feet deep. We have a little space up at the back, where we keep special shells and bits of rock, wedged in with a flat chunk of sandstone so the high-tide sea won't wash them away. But

Lou hadn't gone into the back yet; he was running to and fro at the front of the cave, pointing. There was one line of sneaker prints here too.

I looked at the prints. The person who made them had stopped and peered into the cave, but it didn't look as though he'd gone inside. He was probably too big.

Lou was hooting and gasping; he was really upset. I was afraid he was on the way to one of his seizures. He gets them sometimes if he goes really over the top. Grand says they're a bit like asthma, a bit like epilepsy, though they aren't either one. Nobody knows what they are.

"Lou—stop it, buddy—it's all right!" I went into the cave. I was getting too big for it myself now; I had to go on hands and knees at the back. The wet sand soaked seawater into my jeans.

"Nothing's gone!" I called back to Lou. I could see the chunk of sandstone still in place. I pulled it out, and there safe and sound was the little pile of tritons and whelks, shells you didn't find too often on Long Pond Cay. "Come on in, Lou—come see!"

I knew he'd want to check on his favorite treasure, so I held it up. It was a star shell, about three inches across, the shape of a chunky starfish with ten arms—but it was made of stone. It was a fossil. Lou had found it somewhere or other on the bonefish flats. We'd shown Grand, and he said the shell and the creature inside it had probably been buried for fifty thousand years.

Lou looked into the cave. And then the weirdest

thing happened. As I held up the shell and looked back at him, I heard a long sound that was like the wind in the casuarina trees, but much deeper, longer, far away, as if it came out of the rock. It hummed through the cave, filling the space, louder, louder. And the air around Lou's body seemed to shiver, flickering, the way the air flickers over an outdoor fire as the heat goes up.

Lou stood very still, his head up. I knew he could sense something too. He made a sort of questioning, whimpering sound.

"What is it?" I said. I may be older than him, but he's far better than me at picking things up: at hearing birdcalls or spotting fish, at seeming to know what animals want or say. I put down the star shell and reached out to him.

The sound that was like the wind in the trees echoed through the rock all around us. The air flickered, shaking the edges of solid things. It was scary.

Then it was gone.

Lou took hold of my forearm with both his hands. He was shaking.

"It's okay. Everything's okay." I gave him a hug. Then I showed him the shells, and how they were safe. He put one finger on the fossil shell.

"You want to take it home?" I said.

Lou took his finger away. He shook his head firmly. He liked things to be in their usual places, he didn't like change. So I fitted the piece of sandstone back over the little hoard of shells.

Lou grunted to himself and trotted out of the cave to the beach. I followed him, and we went on along the white sand toward a cluster of casuarina trees, the biggest of which was our special tree. That was where we always sat, on the blanket of brown fallen needles prickled by tiny casuarina pinecones, to eat our sandwiches.

The osprey was sitting in the top of the tree, watching us. We came in very slowly and quietly, settling ourselves on the pine-needle carpet, picking out the prickly cones. Still the osprey stayed there. He knew we wouldn't trouble him. Lou grabbed my backpack and took out the two little plastic bags I'd put there, a peanut butter and banana sandwich in each of them, and the bottle of water. He was hungry and he was very young and I knew he'd already forgotten about the sights and sounds in the cave. That was one of the odd things about Lou: he picked things up fast, but they didn't stay to bother him, they ran out of his mind like water so long as you told him everything was okay.

But I was still bothered. I ate my sandwich slowly, without really tasting it. I kept remembering the weird humming noise, and the flickering of the air. Where did it come from? What *was* it?

Lou gobbled his sandwich and took a long drink from the bottle. He slipped out from under the tree and flung his last crust of bread up toward the osprey, though he knew the big bird would rather have had a fish.

The osprey wasn't interested. He rose majestically

out of the tree and flapped slowly away down the beach.

From somewhere close by we heard an excited shout, and we both looked round.

Three men were standing on the beach about twenty yards away, staring at the osprey, pointing, fascinated. They looked like tourists. They wore dark pants, and shirts with short sleeves, and one of them, the tallest, had a straw hat on his head, with a rainbow ribbon. It looked like one of the hats Grammie's friend Esther sold in the center of town, under the big banyan tree.

The men had cameras strung round their necks, and one of them was holding some sort of instrument on a tripod, and a long cylinder like a fishing-rod case. I didn't think they were fishermen, though. The tall one was trying to watch the osprey through binoculars, but the big hawk flapped away over the water, rising higher and higher.

One of the other men caught sight of us, and waved. They all three came toward us. "Hey, kid!" the man called.

I stood still. I felt suddenly very uneasy, though I didn't know why. It wasn't unusual to find a few tourists on this beach; they came out from town in rented Boston Whalers sometimes, to walk on the sand looking for shells, or to cross the beach to the bonefish flats behind.

Beside me, Lou gave a little nervous grunt.

"Hey, kid!" said the man again, close to us now. He had thick black hair, and big sunglasses hiding his eyes. "You Bahamian?"

"What else would they be?" said the tall man. He had an odd accent I didn't recognize. He took off his hat and fanned his face with it.

I said nothing. Lou began to fidget; I could hear his breathing, getting ominously faster. He was sensing something I couldn't feel. I touched his shoulder, and felt him shaking again.

"These birds, they nest here?" the first man said. "They nest on this island? What is this bird?"

"It's a fish hawk," I said. "I don't know where he nests." I was lying; I knew perfectly well where the ospreys nested, and had been nesting for four years now, but I didn't want tourists disturbing them.

The third man, a skinny guy in a flowery shirt, was standing there looking at me over his sunglasses. He said to the others, "*C'est un petit garçon, ou une petite fille?*"

"*Je ne sais pas,*" said the tall one. "*N'importe, alors.*" Before I could even guess what that was all about, Lou began suddenly to freak out. It was a really bad one. He had been staring at the three men, but now his eyes rolled, and seemed to turn inward. He started grunting, over and over, in a quick rising rhythm, and fighting for breath between grunts. It was a sound I hated, because it scared me. I grabbed him. "Lou—deep breaths—slow down—*deep breaths*—"

The men were staring at Lou as if he were some small dangerous animal. "What's the matter with the kid?"

"*Est-ce qu'il est malade?*"

I reached for Lou's hand, but he took off along the beach, running, stumbling, always making those awful deep unchildlike grunting sounds. I ran after him, calling.

"Lou! Come back! Be still now, be still—!"

I caught up with him pretty soon, round the curve of the beach, in sight of our boat. I grabbed him and held him close to me, talking all the time, telling him to breathe deep, telling him everything was all right, and gradually he began to calm down. That's the only thing you can do with him when he gets like this. Poor old Lou, I wonder what it's like being inside his head; not knowing what's happening to you, and not able to explain it to anyone even if you did know.

He was tired, then, so we got in the boat and went home. There was no sign of the three men, nor of any boat that might have brought them. The tide was rising, the beach narrower than before. Overhead, high up, the osprey was circling, and his mate with him; they wheeled slowly through the sky, and very faintly you could hear their high voices, calling to each other: *peeeu, peeeu* . . .

* * *

Lou was okay by the time we got home. Grand and Grammie were there, in the kitchen. Grammie was mixing up a cake, and she let me have the bowl to lick, and Lou the beater, with a dishtowel under it so he didn't drip. Grand reached out a finger, ran it along the edge of the beater and sucked it absentmindedly, but he wasn't really thinking about cake batter. He had a sheaf of drawings spread out on the kitchen table, and he was scowling at them. Grand has a white fringe of curly beard, even whiter than what's left of his hair, and normally it makes him look picture-book kind and gentle; but when he scowls, his eyebrows join in the middle and the beard juts out ominously.

"Outrageous!" he said, peering at the drawings. "Unthinkable!"

"What's up, Grand?"

Grammie smoothed the batter in her cake pan with a knife. "Have you called the National Trust?" she said to him.

"Calling won't help," Grand said crossly. "I'll go to Nassau."

I put down the bowl and looked over his shoulder. The top page was some sort of plan, with sketches of buildings. "What's the *matter?*" I said.

"Just the death of your favorite place in the world, that's all," Grand said. "Someone applied to develop it. They want to turn it into Miami Beach."

"Develop Long Pond Cay?"

Lou made a small noise, and put down the beater on the floor. Grammie poked him with her foot, and he picked it up again and reached it up to the sink. But he was looking at Grand.

"Look," Grand said. He made room for me to look at the plans. "Look what these idiots want to leave for your generation. Dredge out the channel, bring in fill to build up the beach—and build condominiums all along the bay, with a hotel in the middle."

"You can't build there!" said Grammie, her voice high and upset. "The beach shifts—the first big storm will take it all out!"

"That's not all. Look at this." Grand flipped over two sheets. "Block the tidal inlets, drain the bonefish flats, put in tennis courts and a swimming pool. And a nine-hole golf course!" He turned over another page, and jammed an angry finger down on the next drawing. "And a casino!"

"They can't do that!" Grammie said.

"Oh yes they can, if they get planning permission. You know how they'll sell it to the government—encourage tourism, our biggest industry—boost the out-islands' economy, bring in dollars for the local merchants, create jobs for school-leavers—"

Grammie flopped down on a kitchen chair next to him, as if she were suddenly very tired. "Those people," she said flatly. "They always the same. Any dollars they bring into these islands they take right out again. Most of the money doesn't even come in. Package holidays—the customers pay for them before they leave home, pay their checks right into the bank in America."

"Or in France," Grand said. He held up a glossy advertising folder with a picture on the front of brilliant green palm trees and a bright blue sea. "'Sapphire Island Resort,'" he read. "'Your own private Paradise.' Run by

Offshore Island Enterprises, Fort Lauderdale and Paris. There's a bunch of Frenchmen behind it, I'm told."

I said, "Sapphire Island?"

"Normally known as Long Pond Cay," said Grand.

I looked at the picture. Under the palm trees, a smiling dark-skinned man in a white jacket was bringing a tray with two glasses on it to two light-skinned people in swimsuits. I said, "You can't grow palm trees on Long Pond. There's not enough water."

"They thought of that," Grand said. "They'll have a desalinization plant to make fresh water out of seawater. They'll have sprinkler systems sprinkling it over their palm trees and their golf tees. As for the rest of the golf course, they say they have a special grass that will tolerate salt water."

"I don't believe that," Grammie said. She's a plump, cheerful lady with a round friendly face, but her eyes didn't look friendly now.

"But the government might," said Grand, "if enough experts tell them it's true. What they'll see is foreign capital investing in this island and paying taxes, and not costing them a thing. Not asking for anything except planning permission. We'll just be selling our climate."

"And our beaches," Grammie said. She looked at her cake pan, sitting there full of batter, and got up to put it in the oven.

I felt suddenly cold, in spite of the oven. "Grand—this isn't really going to happen, is it?"

Grand pushed all his papers together. "I don't know, Trey. Some of us going to make as much noise as we can. But these Frenchmen have gone a very long way, very quiet and soft—these are detailed plans, and we only just heard about them today."

I said, "There were three men on Long Pond today who could have been French. They had some sort of measuring instruments with them, and cameras. They were asking where the fish hawks nest, but I didn't tell them."

"No more fish hawks if the bulldozers come," Grand said.

Lou was fidgetting, the way he does when something's upsetting him. He can't keep still then; he moves to and fro like a penned-up dog. He wandered out from the kitchen into the living room, and I saw him squat down near the porch in that suddenly intent way he has. He'd discovered something. He brought it back to show us, opening the palm of his hand to Grammie with a mischievous little grin.

It was a shiny black millipede, curled up into a circle. Lou's loved playing with them ever since he was a baby, and Grammie hates them.

"Oh *Lou!*" she said, as usual. "Let it rest! I wish you wouldn't touch them."

"They don't sting," I said mildly. "Not like centipedes."

Grand said, always the teacher, "They don't need to.

They give off this little whiff of cyanide gas that kills their enemies."

Lou looked interested. He peered closely at his millipede and sniffed it, and Grammie squawked.

"Don't worry," Grand said, "Lou's not their enemy." He stood up, his beard jutting, and held up the papers in his hand. "*These* people the enemy."

THREE

Right after supper that night, my mother telephoned. She always called twice a week, to make sure we were okay, and to check up on things. It may seem odd to you that she didn't live with her children, but the reason was money, and there was no way round it. My parents had split up when Lou was a baby, and my father just took off to live with another lady, leaving Mam with us two children and no money. He'd never sent her a penny from that day to this. So Mam moved in with Grand and Grammie, and got the only job she could find, checking out groceries in the general store in town.

She always wanted to earn more, to help support us, so for four years she spent all her spare time doing a degree course at our island's Resource Centre, where teachers from the College of the Bahamas come to teach people who can't leave home to go to college. When she'd passed her exams she got a much better job in Nassau, and she moved there, to live in a little room in Grand's brother's house.

It was a horrible wrench for all of us, but Mam couldn't find another job on our own island, and we couldn't go with her; Nassau is a big city and a tough place, and she didn't want us kids growing up there. We miss her, but I think she was right; I've been to Nassau twice and I don't like it. Too much stuff going on, too much dirt and noise.

So Mam calls us twice a week, and comes home whenever she can.

"You still fooling around in that boat?" she said, distant in my ear.

"Sure, Mam. Lou loves it."

"You be careful now."

"I always careful. Ask Grand."

Then she said in a different, tighter voice, "Trey, baby, you remember you father?"

"No," I said at once. I felt angry whenever I thought about my father, angry at him for running off with someone else, but I had no real picture of him in my head, and we only had one photograph. It showed him with Mam and me when I was about two. About all you could tell from it was that he was about her same height, and wore a baseball cap, and that his skin was lighter than hers.

I'd always taken care never to wear a baseball cap. I didn't want to be like my daddy.

She said, "I saw him the other day. He wants to get in touch with you, and I said no."

I said quickly, "I don't want to see him, not ever."

"I just wanted to warn you," said my mother's distant voice. It sounded sad, and a bit scared. "You wouldn't ever go off with him, would you?"

"Mam!" I said, horrified. "Of course not!"

"Just watch out. But don't worry. Grand knows all about it. I love you, sweetheart. Is my baby there?"

"Here he is. I love you, Mam." I gave the telephone to Lou, and as he listened he started to smile. They couldn't have a proper conversation, of course, but somehow Mam managed to have long talks with him, all her words punctuated once in a while with a hoot or a little grunt from Lou.

One day about a year ago, Mam had taken Lou to Nassau to see some famous American doctor who was visiting the hospital there. He examined him, and told her there was no physical reason why Lou shouldn't talk. He said it was psychological, and so were his seizures; that something was wrong inside his mind, and that he could probably be put right if she sent him away to live in some special school in the United States.

Mam said no, she'd rather have a quiet little boy who lived at home.

I used to think about that doctor sometimes and wonder if he was right. That was before I found out the things that were so strange and special about Lou, things no doctor would ever be able to understand.

* * *

Three days later, Lou and I went back to Long Pond

Cay. It was our first time together since we'd heard about the developers. You can't get to the cay except by boat, so I knew Lou couldn't have gone there without me unless Grand took him—and Grand had gone off to Nassau with Mr. Ferguson, the high school headmaster, to talk to the government's Lands and Surveys Office about saving the cay from development.

Me, I'd been staying in town for two nights with my friends from school, Lyddie and Kermit Smith. This happened every so often, whenever Grammie decided I needed a change from being way out where we lived— "in the sticks," she put it—looking after Lou. The sticks seemed just fine to me, but that was Grammie, always thinking about ways to improve life for other people. Mrs. Smith was one of her friends from the bank, who said she was always glad to have me because I kept Lyddie and Kermit from killing each other. They were twins, about my age.

I'd asked the Smiths if they had heard about the Frenchman's plans, but they hadn't, and they weren't really interested. They'd never even been to Long Pond Cay—it was way up our end of the island, too far, too isolated.

"We sure could use some development," said Mr. Smith heartily. He was a cab driver. "Jobs. Opportunities. Anything to keep you young people on the island when you finished with school."

"You dreaming, Daddy," Lyddie said.

"Off to Nassau, me," said Kermit. "New York. Los Angeles."

Lyddie grinned at her father. "You'll still have Trey around," she said. "Writing some old book."

I was glad to get back to the sticks, and to Lou.

We went out very early that next time. The tide was going out, but there was still time to get over to the cay before full low. It was a beautiful clear day, and the sky light blue, with a few tiny shreds of cloud that would grow, during the day, into round puffballs drifting in a long row. A pair of whistling ducks flew low over our heads as we puttered up the channel, though they weren't whistling; you could just hear the faint swish of their wings. I was surprised to see them in daylight; usually you see them when it's beginning to get dark. But lots of things were unusual, that day.

We landed, and the beach stretched ahead of us broad and gleaming white, as the tide crept out. Terns swooped in low, calling to each other. We went inland, across the storm-carved slabs of sandstone, through the scrub and the trees, to the lagoon in the center of the cay. The sand there felt different underfoot, soft, squishy, half-mud, with the little spiky shoots of new black mangrove poking up everywhere like nails.

Lou stood staring out at the shallow water of the lagoon, looking for the silvery flash of bonefish, as they butted their heads down into the sand hunting for crabs and shellfish. They feed on the ebbing tide, and again when it begins to come back in. Lou's always loved the bonefish. He can already see a moving school of them quicker than I can. Grand said to me once, "We don't have to worry about him—for all his problems, he'll make a wonderful bonefish guide." And so he will.

But I wasn't thinking about Lou then, just about the fish; like him, I was looking for that dimpling of the water that their tails make as they go headfirst down at the sand, and the quick glint as their silver backs catch the sun for an instant. There were none to be seen, though. The water was too low; it had retreated into gleaming pools and bays left among huge expanses of shining white sand-mud, and the schools of bonefish and snapper had gone out with the tide. Out into the open sea.

It must have been that hour between tides, when the sea is as low or as high as it will go, and everything is sort of suspended, waiting for the turn of the tide.

And then, as I stood there in the silence, looking out over the flats, I thought I saw the air begin to shimmer, blurring the edges of things, as it had that other day in the cave. My heart sank; I didn't want this to happen again. I shook my head and I blinked my eyes hard—but still the shimmering was there, the air wavering as if heat were rising through it.

The wet flats became a shining blur, and the line of palmettos and trees on the opposite side of the lagoon seemed to be reflected in it, double, like a mirage.

And gradually I began to hear that sound again, coming from nowhere, the sound like the wind in the casuarina trees. It grew and grew, rising, whining, filling the shivering air, though when I glanced out of the corner of my eye at a casuarina I saw nothing stir, not a branch or needle move.

The noise filled my head; I wanted to put my hands over my ears. I was so scared that I felt sick. I knew I was on the edge of real panic, and I looked over quickly at Lou.

He hadn't moved. He didn't look the least bit frightened, this time. As I watched, he began to walk slowly forward, over the mangrove-prickled sand, toward the shining stretches of the lagoon. It was a sort of measured walk, not the way a kid moves, and as he went, he did something even stranger, more adult—ancient, even. He raised both his skinny arms into the air, spread wide, as if he were going out to embrace someone.

He stood very still, just stood there, holding his arms out like that. It looked so weird, it sent a chill through me. I moved nervously up toward him, a few slow steps forward.

Then all the sound stopped, and the air wasn't shivering, and there was dead silence.

And out there in the lagoon the water seemed to open, and roll back and disappear. We stood there watching, scarce breathing, and a great shining city rose up before us, growing out of the earth.

It sprang up with a noise like a high wind, a forest of tall towers and cliffs and gleaming straight lines: grey, silvery skyscrapers, scraping the sky. Lou dropped his arms and turned to me; his face was a little boy's face now, frightened, and he grabbed my hand. It was as if he'd become a different person just for a few moments, and now abruptly he was himself again. On all sides the city was springing up, so that the buildings were all around us: we were held in a world of stone and concrete and black brick. Long Pond Cay was gone, and so was the sunlight and the blue sky. The whole world had changed.

FOUR

I stood there with Lou's hand in mine, on a grey concrete paving, in this strange Otherworld city that had swallowed us up as if we lived there, as if we had never lived anywhere else.

No sun shone there; the sky was a grey haze, what you could see of it. The air was very warm, and full of new noise. We were standing on a sort of small paved island where three roads met, two coming up from either side behind us and one stretching out ahead, with cars and buses roaring by us on all sides. I couldn't see a single person walking, anywhere.

Lou let out a high wail of fear. He was clutching my hand with both his own, so hard that it hurt. I looked at his face, all tight with terror, and had no comfort for him because I was in the same state myself. Everything was so different, so suddenly different, that I couldn't think straight. Where were we? What was happening? I wanted to curl up into a ball and hide, until it had all gone away. But I couldn't do that; I was in charge of Lou.

The air felt thick; it caught at my throat. I choked and coughed, but I couldn't hear the sound over the roar of the traffic thundering by. I tried to look at the buses—at least I supposed they were buses: big, sleek silver cylinders full of windows, flashing past in a white blur. Maybe we were in Nassau. Maybe it was New York. Or any big city.

But I'd been in Nassau, and what was going on around us was spookily different from a normal big city. There were no people to be seen anywhere. The cars flashed along in an endless stream, as evenly as if they were on rails, and they all seemed smaller than normal cars, and brightly colored, gleaming red, blue, yellow, orange, green. They rushed by so fast you couldn't see who was driving them.

Over our heads then something came humming loudly, low and fast, and we ducked instinctively. It was a tiny helicopter, much, much smaller than the U.S. Army helicopters that buzz our island every day looking for drug smugglers. I watched it fly away—and then it tilted, paused, curved round and came back toward us. I felt panic rising like a lump in my throat. The helicopter was coming straight at us, and there was nowhere to hide. It paused over our heads, roaring louder than the traffic, and a huge amplified voice came down from it.

"FOOT TRAFFIC BANNED ON THE ARTERY!" it boomed.

I looked frantically up and down the streets. There seemed to be no break anywhere in the moving streams of cars, no way to cross over and escape. The helicopter started coming slowly down toward us.

But at the same time, suddenly a great cloud of black smoke puffed up from the pavement where we stood, swallowing us up. My eyes watered, and I coughed and spluttered, and clutched Lou close to me in alarm—and then, just visible in this dark fog, at our feet a wide disk swung up from the concrete, a kind of cover that I hadn't noticed was there. A man was leaning out of the round hole in the pavement, a bearded man with a black band tied round his forehead, his face anxious and intent. The dark smoke was billowing up out of a kind of cylinder in his hand; he set it down on the concrete and beckoned us.

"Come down, quick!" he shouted over the noise. "Both of you—come down!"

There wasn't time to think; I could feel Lou quivering, and I knew he was on the edge of a terrible seizure. The man looked as scared as I did—that was what made up my mind, I suppose. I pulled Lou over to the hole, and got down so I was sitting on the edge, legs dangling, and the man grabbed Lou into his arms as someone else's hands, down below, took hold of my feet and set them on some kind of ladder. I ducked inside, and the man came down with Lou. In an instant the cover crashed down over our heads and was bolted shut. The air was clear down here, and the roar of the helicopter was muted, shut out.

Lou was whimpering, in the bearded man's arms. "It's

all right, Lou," I said automatically, stupidly. "It's all right—be still!"

But I hadn't the least idea whether anything was all right, or ever would be again.

We were standing in a kind of tunnel, with shiny damp walls lit by dim electric lights that stretched into the distance in a double line. There was a second man beside me, the one who must have grabbed my feet, but he was hidden in shadow.

The bearded man's face relaxed into a big grin. "Beat them!" he said. Suddenly he looked quite different, like a happy pirate. His teeth were very white, and his beard was golden, like the long hair tied down by the black band.

"Let's go!" said the other man, and he pulled forward a big trolley, a flat wheeled thing the size of a small automobile, with a low rim around it like a fence, and a double seat at the front with a steering wheel.

The bearded man put Lou down on the back of the trolley. "Get up, Trey," he said, and I got up, without even wondering how he knew my name. All I could think of at that moment was that they had rescued us from the threat of the helicopter. They made me feel safe. Well, safer. I climbed over the little fencelike side and squatted down beside Lou. The two men jumped into the seat ahead, and we took off quite fast down the tunnel, into the dark. The dim little lights flashed by us like markers. The trolley made a humming noise, not like an engine but loud enough to make it impossible to talk, not that I knew what to say.

We swung round a bend, and I reached out to keep Lou from falling. He let out a long high shriek, a sound that came out of fear and excitement and just letting off steam, and he clutched at me; sat there beside me, clutching my leg.

We went a long way. The air was warm and thick, and drops of moisture splashed down on us from the roof as we rushed along. We seemed to go on for miles, for hours, though I'm sure we didn't. It was like one of those nightmares when something goes on and on, or repeats itself over and over, even though part of your sleeping mind knows that you could change it, if only you could wake up. But you can't wake up.

Then there was light ahead of us, very faint, growing, glimmering on the rounded walls. It was enough to show that we were moving along inside a gigantic pipe, with a bunch of smaller pipes suspended from its roof, running along over our heads.

And then we came round a bend into a big space, where the small pipes all came together and ran up and down in a huge bank, all set about with control wheels and gauges and flickering screens, before taking off again in other directions, along other tunnel-pipes. Lights blazed down from the roof here, as if it was the only important part of this warren, the only part that needed to be seen clearly.

I felt panic beginning to flood through me again.

These people had rescued us from being caught, but where were they taking us? If somebody didn't tell me something soon, I thought my head would explode.

In a corner, shadowed by the bank of pipes, I saw another trolley waiting, with two figures on it. Like our two, they were dressed in rough-looking black pants and tunics, or jackets—either black or very dark colors, I suppose because it made them harder to see, in this strange hidden-away place.

One of them stood up and looked down at us; it was a woman, tall, with a strong-looking dark-skinned face, and a lot of hair that could have been either white or blond, and she was smiling at us, a sunny, warm smile. "Hey babes," she said. "Welcome to the pit, Lou and Trey. And well done, Bryn."

Bryn seemed to be the name of our bearded man. He grinned at her. "Get going, Annie," he said. He looked back down the tunnel.

I couldn't bear this for another minute. "What's happening? *Where are we?*" It came out in a shriek.

The woman put her hand on my shoulder. "Five minutes, and you'll know everything. You're in safe hands in a dangerous place. Get up with them, Gwen. Math, come with me."

The thin man went to join her, and the girl Gwen scrambled up onto our trolley. Then Math's trolley took off and we followed, one after the other, fast; running away. Running away from what?

Over the hum of the trolleys I heard a low booming sound from the tunnel behind us, and I saw all the heads turn anxiously. Both Bryn and Math bent over their controls, but the trolleys were going flat out; they weren't very powerful and this was all the speed they had. In front of me, Gwen made a sudden frightened noise as if she was swallowing a scream, and she whacked Bryn on the leg and pointed back down the tunnel.

I saw a glint of light somewhere back there, and heard a new sound growing. Then the light became a long glitter, and I knew what the sound was, and understood what was following us. It was running water.

Bryn cursed. He looked ahead, and I saw the flicker of a face up there and knew that the others had seen the water too. The sound of it grew, and you could see it gaining on us, a curling grasping wave chasing us down the tunnel, rising, splashing up the sides as it came. "They've opened the sluices!" Bryn shouted to Math.

Math shouted something from the trolley ahead; it sounded like "root hole" and it made no sense to me, but Bryn yelled in agreement and wrenched the steering wheel to one side. I saw a dark ragged gap in the smooth white wall just ahead of us; it was a smaller side tunnel, running off to the right. Bryn turned into it, and Math slowed, swung sideways and came after us.

So did the following wave, splashing at the back wheels of our trolley now. The light dwindled behind us; we were headed into darkness. I held Lou tight. I was sick with fear, imagining the water rising over our heads, rising to the ceiling; feeling myself already suffocating, drowning, trapped like a rat in a drainpipe.

Bryn clicked a switch, and beams of light shone out from the front and back of the trolley. They didn't show much, but you could see that this smaller tunnel was itself rising. The trolley had begun to slow down, but it was going uphill now, and the water wasn't keeping up with it. The wave was still coming after us, but more slowly.

Math called from behind us, "Turn out the lights! It's up ahead!"

There were a few scary moments in the dark, when Bryn turned off the lights, but then you could see a dim glow just visible ahead. This new tunnel wasn't a smooth white pipe; it was carved out of the earth, and we were coming toward a kind of black fringe hanging down from the roof. Bryn steered us underneath it, and paused. He didn't say a word, but I felt the girl Gwen get to her feet as if on command.

Bryn reached up and pulled down a thick line like a black rope, from the dimlit tangle in the opening above us. It swung across the trolley; I felt it brush against my cheek, faintly damp. Gwen grabbed it, as high up as she could reach, brought up her feet to clutch it as well, and hung there like a monkey. She swung to and fro, while Bryn steadied the line, and then she began to climb.

The trolley was beginning to sway beneath us; the water had caught up with it, and we were almost afloat.

Math's trolley was close behind, and he was holding on to ours; only Bryn's hold on the line Gwen was climbing was stopping both trolleys from being washed along by the waves. I stared upward, feeling my heartbeat pounding in my ears. Gwen was disappearing into a scribble of black lines that reminded me suddenly of the casuarina roots on the beach at Long Pond Cay.

Where was Long Pond Cay? Where were we?

Then there was a light patch in the black scribble: it was Gwen's face looking down. Something dropped toward us out of the gap; a kind of rope ladder, two long lines with footpieces joining them.

"Quick!" Bryn said urgently. "You first, Trey, and I'll send Lou after you!"

I hesitated, but I had to trust him; I couldn't send Lou up there in front of me. I grabbed the ladder and got myself onto it, swinging to and fro so wildly that I would have fallen off if Bryn hadn't seized the end, holding it steady.

Lou wailed. I looked down at him. "You come right after me!" I said sternly, and then I climbed up.

And up there, on the other side of the gap, I was in a forest, a world where everything was green. Trees reached high, high all around me, festooned with vines and creepers, and the air was hot, stickily humid, loud with the shrieks of birds. Gwen had hold of my arm, and was pulling me sideways, to stand on firm ground. I bent over the hole through which I'd come, and seized little Lou as he came scrambling up, big-eyed, scared into silence.

Bryn came right after him, and then the woman Annie; they were both looking anxiously down, behind them, and from the hole I could hear the distant roar of running water, and a clashing that must have been the trolleys being flung against each other. There was a desperate shout, and Bryn lunged frantically at the gap. With a great heave he brought Math up, gasping, dripping wet.

Math collapsed onto the mossy ground, among the thick green undergrowth and ginger-smelling dead leaves. He coughed up water, and it gushed out of his nose as well. Bryn whacked him on the back. Lou was holding my arm tightly, watching.

When Math could speak he said, "Where does that one lead?"

"To the sewers," Bryn said. "It was our link between the systems. So in the end it leads out to sea."

"They must have known," Annie said. "They were trying to drown us before we could get out. With any luck they'll think we were washed away."

"We damn near were," Math said. He coughed up more water.

"Rest," Annie said. "Lie there a bit." She stooped and put her hand briefly against his cheek.

We were all standing beside a huge tree, its roots spreading over the ground taller than my head. The undergrowth was so thick and tangled that you could hardly tell where the gap was, the hole through which we'd climbed. I had to peer through the green tangle to see a glimpse of dark space, and hear the rushing water faint below in the tunnel. It wasn't spilling up out of the hole; it rushed on, fierce and fast.

Annie took me by the shoulders with both her hands, and looked down into my face—and into Lou's, close beside me. She said, "This is Pangaia. Very much like the world you know. Very much. Don't be afraid."

Considering we'd just missed being drowned, I thought "Don't be afraid" was pretty funny, but I wasn't feeling like laughing. Her face had the same soft seriousness that Grammie's had, when she was trying to tell me to do better at school, and suddenly I felt very babyish. I said, hearing my voice wobble, "I want to go home."

"You'll be home all too soon," Annie said. "The window stays open only a short time."

"What window?" I said.

She said, "The window between the worlds, when they touch. The way you came here. They'll be watching when you go through—but for the moment they may think you're dead. We must use the time well."

None of it made any sense. I said, "What are you talking about? Who's *they*?"

Lou was watching a big bright yellow moth fluttering round his head; he was smiling, making his happy sound.

"Government," Annie said. "The destroyers."

Lou put out his hand, and the big moth settled on it. But the girl Gwen called out suddenly, loudly, "No!" and she knocked his hand aside.

It was as if the next part happened in slow motion. The yellow moth spiraled down to the ground, turning over and over; its wings dropped off as it fell, floating away like yellow petals, and the soft dark body changed in midair to a gleaming black shape that hit a root and bounced, once, before Bryn smashed his foot down on it. I heard the body crunch under his heel; then when he lifted his foot again I saw the crushed remains of a creature like a gigantic scorpion, with a terrible sting curved high over its back.

Lou stood very still, looking down at it.

Annie said, "That's what they've done. Nothing is what it seems to be."

Gwen patted Lou's shoulder. She was a thin, wiry girl with short curly hair, and older than I had thought at first: eighteen, maybe. "Sorry I hit you," she said. "We wouldn't be here, if we hadn't had to run. Nobody comes here, it's too dangerous. It's the wild land, the Wilderness. Forbidden territory."

"The scientists learned how to change things," Annie said. "Long, long ago. Plants, animals—everything except people. It was genetic engineering, and cloning, to improve the crops we grew and the herds we raised. But it also produced some awful mutations—and those are kept in here, in this high-security Wilderness. Creatures and plants that would never have evolved on their own." She sighed. "It's like everything else they've done! The arrogance! The stupidity!"

Bryn said, "Sit down, Trey. You need to know more than this."

I squatted down on a fallen branch, and he looked down at me with an odd expression, as though he were apologizing.

He said, "We are fighting an underground war, some of us here, against our own kind. Sometimes we call it the Greenwar. The human race is the most powerful that exists, but it is stupid, deaf, blind, and it is killing Pangaia. For gain and greed it has cut down the forests, poisoned the rivers, fouled the air. It pulls down mountains to grind metals out of the rock, it forces rivers to become lakes, to harness the power of the water. Its technology gallops ahead for the sake of more gain and greed—and sometimes, as in this Wilderness, it goes terribly wrong."

Annie said, "You saw the city. That's the image of Pangaia now. The balance of the gases in the air that surrounds this planet has been changed, and the rays of the sun shine through uncontrolled, so that the ice that has covered our poles has begun to melt, changing climates, changing the growth of all green things, changing the level of the sea. In the last fifty years the oceans have risen enough to drown whole cities. Our lowest islands have all disappeared, and the lowest coasts are kept from the waves only by great seawalls. But all the time, the paving of the planet goes on. On they go, our masters, cutting down trees, destroying farmland, building, building, building."

I sat there listening to their quiet angry voices, and it seemed to me that this Pangaia place might just as well be our world, because what they were saying sounded very much like the things Grand complained about all the time. But then I began to hear a difference.

Bryn squatted down beside me, folding his long legs. He picked up a twig and began breaking it absently into little pieces. He said, "So we fight our Greenwar to stop this dance of death, to save our planet from the darkness. Long ago we tried to be reasonable. We pleaded with politicians, we lay down in front of bulldozers, we sang songs. When that didn't work, we tried violence. We blew up the worst polluters we could find: oil refineries, chemical factories and the like. When that didn't work either, we went underground."

"About a hundred years ago, it would be," Annie said.

I blinked at her. "A hundred years?"

"Oh yes. My grandparents' time. We literally went underground—into the labyrinth of tunnels and pipes that makes the underpinning of all these great linked cities. And into the desert lands too, and the forbidden areas, like this one, where normal people don't go. I was born underground. So was Gwen there."

I glanced over at Gwen, who was standing near Math, wringing the water out of his jacket. She looked like a pretty normal teenager to me, not someone born under the ground. She grinned at me.

Lou was sitting very quietly, listening. I wondered what he was making of all this.

Annie said, "And—we came to know Pangaia as our ancestors had known her. We learned to hear. To think. To understand things long, long forgotten. We learned—stories. And prophecies."

She hesitated, and looked over at Bryn, as if she was having trouble saying what she meant.

Bryn got to his feet and came toward me, making me look at him. He said, "Listen carefully to this, Trey. It will sound strange. Pangaia is a planet, but it is also an organism. This whole world. It is made up of everything on it, in it, around it, but it is also a single mind. Its mind is called Gaia. It is a mystery. It will save itself from destruction, it always has. It will save itself from the human race by its own methods—and it plans to use us. We are its agents."

Annie said, "And so are you, and that's why you are here." She was looking at Lou. I didn't know whether I was included in this. Lou gave her his sweet inscrutable smile.

I said, "But what does that mean? What's going to happen?"

"Lou will tell us," Annie said.

I was beginning to think they were all mad. "Lou can't *talk!*" I said.

Math reached up and clutched at Annie's arm, struggling to get to his feet. His lean, lined face looked a bit less pale than before. "We must get on," he said.

Bryn had climbed up onto one of the huge tree roots; his head was constantly turning, looking from side to side, up and down. All around us there were strange unsettling noises, mutterings and whistlings and the occasional distant shriek, and a sound like a continual wind in the trees, though no branch seemed to move.

"Bryn!" Math said sharply. "Can we go?"

Bryn climbed down. A vine had curled itself round his leg, and he ripped it violently away. I could have sworn I heard it whimper.

He said, "Lou will show us the way."

"Lou?" I said. "Are you crazy?"

"The tree will call him," Bryn said.

FIVE

The forest was thick and lush, with high bushes and leafy vines tangling between the trees, and giant ferns and mosses mounded over everything on the ground. Rocks, earth, fallen branches or trees—they were all turned bright green, all swallowed by growing things. Yet it wasn't like any forest I'd ever seen; there was something very spooky about it. Not a glimmer of sunlight came down through the high canopy of branches and leaves; the light was dim, and the air was thick and still and humid. After that one horrific yellow moth, there were no insects to be seen, no butterflies or beetles or wasps or flies, and no birds either. You could hear harsh cries and croakings out there in the trees, but nothing flew or fluttered through the air, or moved on any branch.

As I looked more closely, I began to see that all the trees were exactly the same kind of tree, great spreading giants with broad roots and strange scaly bark, and that the vines were all one kind of vine, thousands of clambering, twining stems, thick as a man's leg and sprouting clusters of broad round leaves. The ferns were all alike too: tall arching fronds as high as my head, with yellow-green leaf-divisions like fingers, the back of each one of them studded with those brown spore-cases you see on most ferns. I put out a finger to touch one, and the thing vanished in a puff of floating brown dust. It smelled bitter, like vinegar.

And Lou walked through all this as if he were following a route he had known all his life.

"The tree will call him," Bryn had said, but what did that mean? The place was full of trees, and trees don't talk. But from the moment those words came out of Bryn's mouth, my little brother Lou stood still, and stiffened, and seemed to forget that anyone else was there. Even me.

He started to move ahead through the forest, slipping through ferns and around trunks and low branches, with such silent certainty that we all followed him. I stayed close behind him, and soon I realized that he had taken us to a kind of path, a clear way through the thick tangled growth that showed no sign of having been cut or cleared, yet was wide enough to let a full-grown man pass through.

Math was at my heels; I glanced over my shoulder and saw him looking ahead at Lou intently, out of his bright dark eyes. I also saw, for the first time, that the handle of a big knife was sticking out of the top of one of his close-fitting boots. The boots were still soaked with water; it was the faint squishing sound that had made me look down at them.

In that same moment, everything around us erupted. Lou leaped back, yelping, Math's hand flashed down and up, and the knife was flying through the air to bury itself, ahead, in something black and furry and snarling, blocking the path.

Lou fell, and I grabbed him. Bryn and Annie were diving forward, past me: "Get back!" Annie hissed at me. "Keep him back!" And I saw they had knives too, and were striking like Math at the thing ahead, again and again, grunting, intent.

The thing screamed, a horrible high shriek, and then it was silent and still.

Math brought his knife down in one last violent slash, and a spray of liquid came flicking back at us. When I wiped it off my arm I saw that it was blood.

The creature looked like a rat, the size of a dog. It had a pointed nose and a long hairless tail, and its body was sleek black. It lay there, filling the pathway. The jaws were stretched wide and menacing, full of huge sharp yellow teeth. There was blood everywhere. I held Lou close; I knew he must have been terrified.

But Lou was wriggling out of my hands, not shaking, not trembling on the edge of a seizure, not even visibly afraid. He was looking ahead. He had his head up as if he was listening. He gave a little gurgle that was almost like his happy sound, and he kept on going, walking round the path and the twitching body of the giant rat.

"Lou!" I shouted.

"Just follow him," Annie said in my ear. "He can hear the tree."

"*What tree?*" I said unhappily.

The others were passing us, following Lou. Annie held me back. "Listen to me," she said. "In your world, Lou is nothing, but in ours, he is magical, he is predestined. We have been waiting for him. Only he can save this world, only now and only here."

I couldn't make sense of any of this. "I have to look after him! I always have—he's my little brother, it's my job."

"It's still your job," Annie said. "But it's ours too." She gave me a big warm smile, that lit up her face like sunlight, and tugged my hand so that we were running together to catch up with the rest. The shrieking in the trees grew suddenly louder, and in a great flapping flurry a big dark-colored bird swooped over our heads and away again, into a tree. I couldn't see it clearly. It looked a bit like a golling, a bird we have in the islands that's the size of a duck, and usually comes out only at night. But this one was far, far bigger.

"It's harmless," Annie said. "Keep going."

"They're all huge. Everything."

"Mutants." We'd caught up with the others; I could see Lou trotting purposefully ahead of them. "That's why Government preserves the Wilderness—to study them. There's a big research facility somewhere in here, and the whole area's shut off, and guarded. It's a bad place, the Wilderness. If it didn't have some of the oldest trees on the planet, we'd have attacked it long ago."

With a swoosh, the dark bird flapped back across the path over our heads, and then into the trees again. It didn't seem able to fly very high. Bryn and Math looked up uneasily, but little Lou paid no attention; he went on, without pausing. The forest seemed a bit brighter here, as if more light was filtering down through the thick crisscross of branches overhead. There were fewer trees too. Gradually, as we went on, the light grew, and I began to see a few chinks in the green ceiling, a few glimpses of hazy sky. We were beginning to come out of the forest.

And then, in an instant, we were out of it, and all of us stopped, bumping into each other like a line of dominoes. We were standing on a slope, there among the few remaining trees, and spread before us was a grey world of concrete and steel and stone, an unbroken city, stretching as far as we could see in all directions. Buildings and streets filled an enormous plain, flat, flat, until in the distance it rose into slopes like the one on which we stood. Beyond them, folds of hills rose higher and higher, each of them grey with the buildings of the city, until they vanished into a brown haze.

Gwen was standing beside me now, looking out. "There is what we've done to Pangaia," she said bleakly. "There's our world."

Lou had paused only for a second. He was standing there now on the mossy slope, turning his head from side to side, like a dog casting about for a scent. Then he began to move again, sideways, toward a rocky outcropping surrounded with the same tall ferns that had crammed the floor of the forest. And I saw that beyond the rocks, between the forest and the endless sprawl of the city, a tremendous steel-mesh fence stood as a barrier, topped with whorls of barbed wire. Beyond it was a second fence, just as big, just as sturdy, and beyond that a third. If Lou's strange convinced sense of direction was leading us all toward the city, we'd have a hard time getting there.

We followed Lou, walking now over stony ground patched with moss and clumps of an odd yellow grass. I was staring out at the fences, which looked taller and more forbidding the closer we got to them. I said to Gwen, "How can we possibly get out of here, with those in the way?"

She said, "If the tree is inside the fence, just be grateful we're here. It would have been even harder to get in than to get out."

There was that word again. *"What tree?"* I said.

Then gradually I began to hear, somewhere, a sound that seemed to come straight from Long Pond Cay: a weird husky whistling sound like the wind in the casuarina trees. It was soft but unmistakable, and though it didn't grow louder, it didn't go away. It seemed to fill the air all around us; I couldn't tell where it was coming from.

Lou walked round the group of tall irregular rocks ahead of us on the slope, and as we followed him I could see an inner cluster of rocks with a tree growing out of them. Its roots were spread over one flat rock like long dark fingers. It wasn't very big, maybe twenty feet high, but it looked very, very old; its trunk was broad and twisted, with grey bark smooth as stone, and its thick, gnarled branches drooped, as if they had carried a heavy weight for a long time. They were covered all over with new side-shoots and twigs bearing long thin leaves almost like pine needles. And all these were moving in a breeze that I couldn't feel; a breeze that came from nowhere, and blew only on this one tree, producing that soft moaning casuarina sound that was filling the air. It was like singing, though it had no words.

Perhaps it had words for Lou. He paused, and clambered up onto a ledge of rock on the way to the tree. Bryn and Math climbed up after him—and then they both gave a kind of strangled gasp, and grabbed fast for their knives, staring downward. Gwen and Annie and I scrambled up to look over the edge of the rock.

It was like a snake pit, all round the tree. Between the outer group of great lichen-patched boulders where we were standing, and the rocks in the middle where the tree grew, there was a gap like a big ditch, filled with shiny black bodies, moving, slowly rippling, like a sluggish sea. They were hideous: thick armor-plated cylinders about three feet long, with tiny snout-like heads. At first they looked like stubby hard-shelled snakes, but after a moment you could see the legs, hundreds of legs, moving ceaselessly under each body. There was a very faint smell that reminded me of something, though I couldn't remember what.

Bryn was looking down in fascinated disgust. He took a breath, and I saw his fingers tighten round his knife. He said to Math, "If we go down together, back to back, we can cut a way through."

But Math didn't have a chance to answer. Lou swung round in front of them, making the throaty noises that for him were "No, no!" He was shaking his head violently, and he had his hands up, trying to push them both backwards, away from the ditch.

Math looked down at him in astonishment. He said, "What, then?"

Lou put his finger to his lips. He held up the other hand with its palm toward them. Then very slowly he began to edge himself down into the pit full of those squirming black monsters.

"Ah, no!" Math said, appalled. He started forward, and Lou stopped, frowning, and held up his hand again.

"Let him be," Bryn said. "He knows what he wants to do."

And just as I began to panic, I remembered in an instant where I had first smelled the faint smell that was in the air here. It was the tiny hint of a scent that you could catch once in a while from one of Lou's favorite

playthings at home on the island: the little black millipedes, that grossed out Grammie but curled obligingly
into a harmless circle in Lou's gentle fingers.

I stared down at the pit. These awful-looking things,
long as my leg, were gigantic mutant versions of Lou's
millipedes. He seemed to have recognized them at
once—but would they recognize him? I had a sudden
terrible vision of him down there, screaming, covered
with flailing black bodies.

Lou looked up and caught my eye, and shook his
head. He grinned. He knew just what I'd been thinking.

Then he climbed slowly down into the ditch, and
squatted at the edge of the mass of black bodies. He
reached down and patted one of them; then knocked on
its hard black back with his knuckles, and laughed.

The millipede curled itself slowly into a circle. So did
the next, and the next. And on, and on, until every one
of them was curled up like an automobile tire, lying there
unmoving, unthreatening, in a harmless heap.

"I'll be damned," Bryn said.

Lou laughed again, and he walked across the ditch,
stepping lightly from one black curled body to the next,
until he reached the other side. He paused, and looked
up at the tree.

He was still my little brother, and he was alone. I said
softly, "Lou? Shall I come?"

He smiled, but he shook his head, and looked up at
the twisted old tree above him. He reached up, and put

his hand on the trunk. All this time the strange wind that nobody could feel had been singing softly through the thin needle-like leaves, in a constant background, rising and falling a little but never stopping. I could hear it, I could see the leaves moving, but I could feel no breath of wind at all.

Lou was listening intently; you could see the concentration on his face.

I said softly to Gwen, hesitating a bit because it sounded so ridiculous: "Uh—is the tree talking to him?"

"Of course," she said, and she gave me a smile so open and cheerful that it was like a hug.

"Well—what's it saying?"

"Nobody knows that but Lou," she said.

We all stood there watching Lou and the singing tree, bemused, and in the background, beyond the steel fences, the silent grey city stretched to the horizon in all directions.

Then the pitch of the tree's singing changed, grew higher, shrill, and Lou looked up suddenly at the sky, alarmed. A louder noise came roaring toward us, and down over the tall fences came two whirring helicopters like the one that had dived at us when we first found ourselves in the Otherworld. They were small, black and sinister, and they moved very fast. Before we could gather our wits they were hovering low over the ground near the rocks, and a real wind was whirling dust and leaves through the air, turning us all blind and deaf for a scrambling moment. The noise was painful. A figure dropped to the ground from each helicopter: two men in dark red jumpsuits, some kind of uniform. The helicopters rose again instantly, to hover higher up.

I found myself knocked sideways, rolling, caught then by Annie's outstretched arm. All four of them had dived behind the outer row of boulders, taking me with them.

"Police!" Gwen hissed in my ear. "Keep behind the rock!"

"But Lou—!"

Bryn put his hand over my mouth and said in my ear, "We'll get Lou. Just watch."

The two policemen, quick and intent, were running toward the rocks, toward Lou and the tree. We lost sight of them for a moment and then they reappeared on the edge of the outer circle of rocks, facing the ditch. They paused, uncertain, looking down at the sea of giant millipedes, piled still in mounds of shiny black coils. Even without movement, the sudden sight must have been awesomely nasty.

Lou was standing beside the tree, his hand on its trunk, watching them. One of them called to him. "Hey kid—you're in danger! Come on out of there!"

Lou shook his head. He waved to them, smiling. I couldn't believe how cool he was. Then he patted the trunk of the tree, almost as if he were telling it something, and he walked away from it, away from the men, toward the end of the inner group of rocks, facing us.

One of the men yelled at him again, and took out something that looked like a gun, but the other knocked his hand down. The first man put the gun away and began, reluctantly, to clamber down into the ditch toward the silent millipedes. The other followed him. And two things happened at once, very fast, so fast that I couldn't believe what I was seeing.

The instant both men were in the ditch, all the giant millipedes uncoiled, whipping their bodies straight, moving in absolute unison as if they were a school of fish. They seemed suddenly much bigger. Their snouty little heads were up, facing the two policemen. And both the men dropped like stones, and a second later, that strange isolated wind sprang up over the ditch, whirling the branches of the tree, blowing away from us, away from Lou.

The millipedes swarmed slowly but relentlessly over the two bodies, covering them, but I knew the men had been dead the moment they fell. I'd been hearing Grand's voice at the back of my memory, talking about the little black creatures we have at home. *They don't sting—they don't need to. They give off this little whiff of cyanide gas that kills their enemies. . . .*

Not such a little whiff, when the millipedes became giants. And when the cyanide had killed the enemies, that wind had sprung up to blow it away from the friends.

The sound of the helicopter engines grew louder again. Lou looked up. He was such a small unlikely figure there, in his T-shirt and shorts and raggedy sneakers.

Overhead, the two helicopters were dropping out of the sky again toward us; they must have seen what had happened to the two policemen.

"Run, Lou!" I shouted desperately, though he couldn't have heard me.

He slid into the ditch and patted the nearest of the giant millipedes on its shiny black back, just as he had at first, and then rapped on it lightly with his knuckles. And just as before, the creature curled itself obediently into a tight circle, and so did the next, and the next. As soon as there were enough of them to make a pathway across the seething black mass, Lou ran toward us, jumping from one coil to the next as if they were stepping stones. Bryn and Math pulled him out of the ditch as soon as he was across.

"Quick!" We were all running back to the forest, as the helicopters dropped lower and lower.

But the police seemed less interested in us than in the tree, the small ancient tree among the rocks, that had sung to Lou. The two helicopters hovered low over it for a moment. Then from each of them a brilliant ray of light flicked out, focusing on it, and instantly the whole tree was in flames. Every inch of its black trunk and branches and roots was glowing orange, licked with white flame; and then the rays flashed again, reaching down around it, into the ditch.

Lou stopped in his track, looking back, and suddenly he was a seven-year-old again. He let out a high wail, and Bryn scooped him up and carried him off under his big arm.

I kept glancing over my shoulder as I ran. Again and again those two rays of light, or laser, or whatever they were, stabbed down from the helicopters at the blazing tree. They were surely determined to finish it off. Or maybe they were simply using it to fry the millipedes.

We had reached the shelter of the edge of the forest, where the shadow began. Lou struggled down from under Bryn's arm, and took my hand. We turned to look back at the tree, with its two attackers hovering still, like great roaring armor-plated dragonflies. Beyond the flames you could see the tall steel-mesh fence rearing up, and in the distance the grey blur of the city, under the hazy sky.

As I looked, I realized that everything I saw was quivering. It was that shimmering of the air that we had seen before, a little and a long while ago. I thought at first it was the heat from the flames, but then I heard the sound that had come with it, that first time, the sound like the sighing of the wind through casuarina pines. It rose, and grew shrill, drowning out even the roar of the helicopters' engines. Perhaps it was the last message from the dying tree.

Lou clutched my hand very hard.

Then the sound dropped away.

There was no haze over the sky now; it was clear blue. A breeze was blowing round our bodies, and we were breathing cooler air. Sunlight shone all around us, bouncing up from white sand and clear water. We were standing on Long Pond Cay, facing the flats, all shining and still with a tiny line of silver-top palms on the horizon. I could feel the seawater oozing into my sneakers. The wind breathed softly in the casuarina trees behind us, and under it was the slow rhythmic whisper of the sea.

The still water of the great inland lagoon before us was dimpled by the upturned tails of bonefish, flashing silver as they dug their noses into the muddy bottom, hunting for food. Small ripples walked across the surface, echoes of the waves out at sea. The tide was coming in.

SIX

When we came home, to Grammie calling us to make ourselves clean and tidy for supper, I realized that we'd been gone only for that one suspended hour between the falling and the rising of the tide. However long our time in the Otherworld had seemed to us, it was barely sixty minutes of real time, the time of our own world. I felt dazed, as if I'd been deep asleep for a long time and hadn't properly woken up yet.

Lou was completely himself again, a bouncing hungry seven-year-old, flinging his arms round Grammie's broad waist as she stood at the kitchen counter slicing summer squash. She wiped her hand automatically on her apron and patted his curly black head.

"You had a good day, then?"

"Fine," I said. "Saw a big eagle ray in the cut, coming back."

The huge diamond-shaped fish had coasted lazily beneath our boat, flapping its spotted sides like wings.

"Good luck sign," Grammie said cheerfully. "So long as you don't step on him."

"Is Grand back?"

"He still in Nassau. Staying with his brother. They got appointments with Government." She sighed, and reached for another squash. "Much good that going to do. You see anything happening over to Long Pond Cay?"

"No," I said. I looked down at Lou, and he gave me a small private smile. I knew that if Grand had been home, I might at that moment have tried to tell him about everything that had happened. But not Grammie. She was far too practical. "Child, you got too much imagination," she'd say.

And so I have, but that's not where the Otherworld came from.

I had trouble falling asleep that night. There were too many memories crowding through my head, too many sounds and sights and smells. And there was Lou, my different little brother who was in fact far more different than I could possibly have imagined.

I looked across at his bed, where this small skinny boy lay fast asleep, breathing quietly and evenly. *"In our world, he is magical, he is predestined,"* Annie had said. *"Only he can save this world."*

One thing was for sure. Sooner or later we would find ourselves in the Otherworld again. And then what would happen?

When Grand did come home, next day, he was fit to

be tied. The group of French and American developers calling themselves Sapphire Island had been making their plans for months, perhaps years. They had applied for all kinds of official permissions, perfectly legally, while nobody on our island had any idea of what was happening, and they'd been granted most of them. Pretty soon, they would begin making changes on Long Pond Cay.

They would destroy it, Grand said. He took me into town for the weekly shopping expedition at the market, where he bent the ear of anyone who would listen. There's only one big market, so everyone goes there sooner or later—and they all know Grand. He stood just outside the door, where there's a convenient patch of shade from the roof, and carried on to a group of his friends.

"It's criminal!" he said. "They buying our land! This the whole state of the islands, in a nutshell—of the whole Caribbean!"

"Tell it like it is, James!" said Jerry Salt from the liquor store. He's a tall man with muscles, and dreadlocks. He patted Grand on the back.

Grand fixed him with a cold eye. "You know Long Pond," he said. "You and my boy went there all the time. It's all one system—beaches, land, sea, creeks, mangroves, sea grass, fish, birds—all one ecosystem. We all part of it. But it's Nature, it's got to be free to go its own way. That western shoreline changes shape every month. If these people try to fix it solid, the whole ecosystem going to die."

"They bringing in a dredge next week," said Mr. Wells, who worked for the telephone company. "Gonna dredge the creek and the lagoon."

I thought of that great peaceful stretch of water in the middle of Long Pond Cay, the lagoon where the bonefish drift in to feed on the changing tides, and chills went down my spine.

"Birds nest there," Grand said. He thumped one hand into the palm of the other. "Young fish shelter there. Conch breed there. All that going to go, if they build a harbor, a hotel, a *casino!* A place just for people is no place at all."

"Right on!" said Jerry Salt.

"Yeah!" said a couple of teenagers, but they were grinning and I didn't think they meant it.

A sunburned American with a blond ponytail said quietly, "Long Pond sure is a beautiful spot." He wore raggedy shorts and a T-shirt. He was probably one of the boat people.

Grand pulled a piece of paper out of his little canvas briefcase. It was a notice he'd carefully printed out from his computer the night before. "I putting this up in the market—there's a meeting in the community center this Friday. Seven o'clock. We starting a petition to Government, to save the cay. Come! All of you come!"

They all nodded their heads, and we went into the market. It took a long time to get the groceries, because Grand started all over again, talking to everyone in there too.

Lou and I went to that meeting, partly because I begged Grammie to let us, and partly because Grand needed me to work the slide machine. I knew how to do that, from school, and Grand had all kinds of pictures of Long Pond Cay that he wanted to show. Photography was his hobby, and he'd been taking wonderful nature photographs for years, underwater as well as on land. They were really good slides, of everything and everybody that lived on the cay: terns, nighthawks, plovers, oyster-catchers, kingbirds, our pair of ospreys; then under the sea: sharks, barracuda, rays, mullet, snapper, bonefish, crabs, shellfish—even the little round jellyfish that live on the shallow bottom, green-fringed with weed. Lou and I used to throw those jellyfish at each other when we were younger, when Grand wasn't looking.

The slides went on and on: palmetto, mangrove, buttonwood, bay cedar, sea grape, sea oats, seven-year apples, casuarina pines . . . lizards, hermit crabs . . . everything except people. No people lived on Long Pond Cay. Yet.

There were plenty of people at the meeting, though. Local people, from the high school headmaster and some clergymen, the doctor and the dentist, on down to ordinary folks like us, and a few retired Americans and English people who had houses on the island. There were a bunch of boat people from cruising yachts too, Americans and Canadians mostly, though this was summer and most of the boats come in winter and spring. The man with the blond ponytail was there, in a clean shirt and pants this time. "Just want you to know that anything you want us to do, we'll do," he said to Grand. "We come to these islands to get away from development, not to watch it eating up the wild places."

He was a nice man, I think, and I could tell that Grand liked him, but it was this same blond American who was the cause of the trouble in the end, without intending it. The meeting started, and Grand gave a very persuasive talk, clicking his fingers at me whenever he wanted a slide changed. I managed to get them all in the right order at the right time, except at the very end, when I found them starting all over again from the beginning.

"No—someone else's turn now," said Grand. Everyone laughed, and Mr. Ferguson our headmaster took over.

All the speeches said the same kind of thing, about how Long Pond Cay was a special untouched precious place, where birds and fish and all the other wild things were able to live free, all of them depending on each other. It was okay for people to walk on the beach, they said, and for the bonefishermen to come in their boats, because these people just stayed for a little while and then went away again. But if anything were to be built on Long Pond, even a few houses, the whole ecosystem would be changed. And if a huge development like Sapphire Island came there, digging out the shallow lagoon and creeks and covering the sandy flats with concrete, the whole wilderness would die.

I knew just what they meant. I thought of walking barefoot with Lou over the soft mud-sand beside the lagoon, with mangrove shoots prickling between our toes, and silence all around us except for a few terns peeping, and the occasional small splash of a fish. And just for a moment, a picture of the endless grey city of the Otherworld flashed into my mind.

Mr. Ferguson said Long Pond Cay was a heritage that should be preserved and passed on to my generation. He said this would be true for us too when we grew up, that it was true for all generations, and he quoted old Chief Seattle, the American Indian.

> *"This we know:*
> *The earth does not belong to us*
> *We belong to the earth. . . ."*

One of the clergymen, I don't know his name, said that God gave us our islands in trust, and we had to look after them. Our local member of the government got up then, and said yes that was absolutely true, but we must also invest our talents wisely, and not bury them like the man in the Bible story. He was being careful not to offend anyone, I think, so he ended up not saying much on either side, for or against Sapphire Island Resort.

But after him, a friend of Grammie's called Mrs.

Ernestine stood up, a tall portly lady with a church hat and a big voice, and she made a very fiery speech about the islands being for the islanders, and not just a playground for rich white foreigners to gamble and play golf.

"We hear this big talk about investment!" Mrs. Ernestine cried. "Who investing in what? Big foreign companies investing in *us*, in our pretty beaches and our blue sea, that's what, and taking they profits home to they own countries to enjoy! Long Pond Cay belong to us—Sapphire Island would belong to them! Let's sign our petition, people, and show the Government how we truly feel!"

We all cheered, and Mrs. Ernestine sat down, looking pleased, and fanned herself with her hat.

The blond American got up next, which was brave of him considering he was a foreigner. He spoke rather softly, so you had to strain to hear him, but he was worth hearing. He said he thought he was a typical boat person, or "yachtie," and that there were hundreds like him in our waters every year.

"We're an independent lot, but we all love these islands," he said. "We come here for several months of the year to escape from noise and bustle. We're trying hard now not to pollute the water of your harbor. We used to be bad about that, but we've listened to people like Mr. Peel—"

—that was Grand, and I nudged Grammie proudly—
"—and we've learned." He looked round him a little

nervously, but his voice rose. He said, "I think your government has to learn too, to limit large-scale development, and allow only small hotels, on islands big enough to support them. Long Pond Cay is beautiful and peaceful, and part of the reason why we all come here. Sapphire Island Resort doesn't belong there."

People clapped when he sat down, but almost at once another man bounced to his feet and started yelling, a loud angry yell. He was Bahamian, but I didn't recognize him, I thought he must be from one of the outer settlements. He was a big man with a shiny bald head and two chins, and a yellow shirt. He started right in on the boat guy.

"You don't belong here neither!" he bellowed. "What you know about us? You sit out there on your million-dollar boat, you go catching our fish, you don't do nothing for this island—we need jobs, man! Big hotels, not small little hotels! We need investment in our economy! We need money for better roads and better schools!"

Some people began to get caught up in this, and to shout "Yeah!" at intervals.

"We need jobs and Sapphire Island goin' give us them!" the fat man shouted. "Let me tell you, they goin' rebuild the main road!"

"Yeah!" shouted the people around him.

"Let me tell you, they goin' help expand the airport!"

"Yeah!"

"Let me tell you, they goin' hire drivers and construction workers and hotel staff and all kinds of jobs! How many people here goin' say no to one of those jobs, eh? You show me your hand if you goin' say no to a job—"

And the meeting fell apart, as he bellowed on, and people jumped to their feet to bellow back at him, and Grand tried in vain to shout for order. At the end, the best we could do was to stand at the door of the community center with copies of the petition, and try to get people to sign as they left. Maybe half of them signed.

"We'll collect signatures on Sunday after church," I said to Grand on the way home, trying to cheer him up. "We'll get a whole lot more!"

We were all squished in the cab of his truck, Grammie sitting silently beside me with Lou asleep on her lap. Grand took a long heavy breath, and let it out again.

"It goin' get harder than we imagine, Trey," he said. "That man was from off-island, I never saw him before. They brought him in to stir things up, and tell lies. It a lie about rebuilding the road, and extending the airport— Sapphire Island not doing any such thing. They won't hire many workers from this island either, they'll bring skilled labor in from outside. All they *will* do is pave over our land, and ruin our waters, and develop all the life out of Long Pond Cay."

"But we'll fight them!" I said.

Grand lifted his chin as he drove through the darkness, and his beard jutted again. "Oh yes," he said. "We'll fight."

* * *

The petition took over our lives for a few days after that. Everyone who was against the Sapphire Island development took to the roads, or hovered outside shops and restaurants, collecting signatures and arguing. The list of signatures grew longer and longer. The blond American put together a separate petition for the boat people, because they weren't Bahamian citizens. He specially wanted to find boat owners who were scientists or experts in pollution, so that they would be offering the government advice worth taking seriously. You could see him buzzing round the harbor every day from boat to boat in his grey inflatable dinghy, with his equally blond wife.

The news of the petition even reached Nassau, and a reporter from one of the newspapers came out for the day to interview Grand and Mr. Ferguson and the rest. She had a camera, and she came to the house and took pictures of Grand and Grammie in among the banana trees on the farm. It was a good year for bananas; we were going to have a handsome crop. She wanted to have Lou and me in the pictures too, but Lou got very upset and was on the edge of having a seizure, so I took him away.

Lots of people didn't agree with Grand and his friends, and some just didn't seem to care. "Don't ask me, man," said one young man coming out of the liquor store. He was a dude, with a big gold chain round his neck. "I ain't signing no petition. What I care about Long Pond Cay? I never go *near* that end of the island."

Grand couldn't resist arguing with people like that, trying to make them face responsibility, and sometimes he succeeded in shaming one of them into adding his name to the list. But he never got far with Mr. Smith, the father of my friends Kermit and Lyddie, who was firmly in favor of Sapphire Island and any other kind of development. Whenever they passed in the street, Mr. Smith would lean out of the window of his cab and call, "Opportunity, Mr. Peel! Got to face the future! Can't let opportunity pass our children by!"

Grand would mutter crossly to himself, "Opportunity for who?"

When they had almost as many signatures as they felt they could get, Grand and the other organizers managed to persuade someone in government to see them, and they flew to Nassau again. Grammie drove him to the airport in the truck, and Lou and I went too. "Good luck, Grand," I said in his ear as I kissed him good-bye. "Please save Long Pond."

Grand smiled at me. "You save those bananas from the birds, and I'll see what I can do," he said.

But I couldn't save the bananas, though it wasn't the birds I had to worry about.

The morning after Grand left, Lou and I went up early to the farm, to scare birds and do some weeding. We took sandwiches and water, so we wouldn't have to come back for a while. The farm's a big piece of cleared land about fifteen minutes' walk from our house, with a fence round it to keep the goats out. It's in a kind of broad hollow, where the soil is good, though there's scrubland all round it. Nobody lives nearby, so it has to be checked every day to make sure we get the things that are ready to be picked, before the birds do. We had two sacks with us for the tomatoes, because they were doing really well; Grammie got a great price for them at the market.

The path to the farm winds about a bit, through scrubby bushes and big trees, and Lou was running ahead of me. I was carrying a hoe and a machete, so I wasn't about to race him. I saw him reach the last bend before the banana trees began—and then he suddenly stopped, as if he'd run into a wall. He stood quite still for a moment, staring, and then he looked back at me and began to give a long high wail.

I came up to join him, and looked.

The farm looked as if it had been hit by a hurricane. There was nothing left standing. The banana trees, the papayas, the tomato plants, all the other fruits and vegetables that Grand had tended so carefully, were all lying flat on the ground. Nobody had stolen the fruit—it was lying there on the ground, spoiling. This hadn't been done by thieves, but by a determined person with a very sharp machete. You could see the marks where the blade had sliced through the thick trunk-like stalks of the banana trees, and the big hollow stems of the papayas.

We clambered about, through the ruins of the plants and bushes. Lou was making little whimpering sounds now. He patted some of the fallen trees as if they were wounded pets. Looking at it all, I began to feel anger growing like a big lump in my chest, almost like a pain. I wanted to whack at whoever had done all this, to chop at him with his own machete.

Perhaps there had been more than one person. Perhaps two or three. They had done a very thorough job. Big feet had trampled all the young cabbages into the ground, and kicked holes in pumpkins and squash. The only things they'd left were the onions, which were under the ground and harder to hurt, and the pigeon pea bushes at the edges of the farm plot. But pigeon peas aren't valuable; everyone grows them.

I said to Lou, "Let's pick up all the tomatoes we can. Even the green ones—Grammie will make chutney." I knew I had to telephone Grammie at the bank as soon as I could, but she wouldn't have arrived there yet. So we filled our bags with tomatoes, and my lump of anger kept growing, especially when I looked across at the banana trees. There had been two or three big hands of bananas on every tree, but only half-grown yet, still small and green. The whole crop had been lost.

I called Grammie when we got back to the house. I was spluttering with rage, but she was quiet. "Oh my," she just said, at first. "Oh my." Then she told me we should go on rescuing what we could, and by the time we had gone back and filled our bags with tomatoes and green papayas a second time, a black police jeep came bumping along the trail to the plot, with a policeman inside it, and Grammie.

She got out, in her good bank dress and her good shoes, and Lou ran to her and clutched her.

"Lou and Trey," she said, "this is Constable Morgan. He a good friend of your mother's. I knew him when he was your age. He kindly came to inspect our poor farm."

She looked at the mess, and I saw her chin quiver.

Constable Morgan had a perfectly round face, and his eyes grew even rounder as he peered at the splintered bushes and fallen trees. "Oh Lord," he said. "Somebody sure had it in for you, Mistress Peel."

There was nothing he could do, of course. No witnesses, no evidence, just a lot of ruined fruit and vegetables. He helped us pick some more tomatoes, and squash and green peppers, and Grammie sent him back to the police station with a bag of them for his wife.

Grand said, when he came home from Nassau, "Looks like somebody sent me a message. Stop making noise, James Peel, if you know what's good for you."

"Will you stop?" I said.

Grand smiled a little. "Child," he said, "I gonna shout my big old head right off."

Grand and his friends had managed to reach the right minister in government, armed with their petition, and they had a small success. Because the Sapphire Island Resort people were outsiders, and the petitioners all Bahamian, the minister put a one-month stop on development until she could look more closely at the whole case.

"But these people got good lawyers, and powerful arguments," Grand said. "Now we have to work even harder."

So the collecting of signatures went on, and there were more meetings, and posters began appearing all over the island, on walls and doors and tree trunks, saying, SAVE LONG POND CAY! Grand was spending all day and every day in town, or at his computer, organizing the protest. He did arrange for a couple of men to come in and clear up the damage at the farm, and Lou and I hung out with them to help, and watch them burn the trash, making a great plume of grey-white smoke.

Grand was leaving the running of his bonefishing business to other people too, for the time being, but all his bonefish guides were good men, and his chief guide, Will Torris, was one of his oldest friends. Besides, this was summer, and most of the visitors came to fish later in the year.

We liked Will; he was a tall, stooped man with a big quick smile and enormous hands and feet. But those big hands could tie the smallest fly onto a bonefish line, and he and Grand had been teaching us all we knew about fish and the sea and the islands, ever since we were babies. Lou and I kept our little dinghy down at an old jetty alongside the bonefish hut, with its smart little marina for the nine boats, and Grand and Will's office under the neatly painted sign, JAMES PEEL: BONEFISHING.

Lou was restless; I knew he wanted to go out in the dinghy. We both missed the water if we hadn't been out there for more than a few days, or gone over on Long Pond Cay. But on the day I intended to go, Will Torris turned up at the door early in the morning, just as we were having breakfast.

I said, "Hi, Will!" through a mouthful of cereal, but he didn't hear me; he was looking at Grand, very serious.

"James," he said.

Grand offered him a mug of coffee.

Will shook his head, holding up his big hand. "James," he said again, and stopped.

"What is it?" said Grand. He put down the coffee mug.

Will said unhappily, "Four of the boats are gone."

"Gone?"

"Chains cut. Completely gone. All nine of them were there last night, tied up, chained up, batteries clipped down. I checked them myself. Somebody took four. Must have had good tools—the chains were cut through like butter. I sorry, sorry, James!"

"Good grief, it's not your fault," Grand said. He put his arm over Will's broad shoulders, and they went out, down to the bonefish hut, followed by Grammie and me, and Lou hopping about like an agitated frog. Lou ran to our dinghy the moment we got there; I think he was more worried about that than about Grand's fine boats, which were all a special design he'd bought the year before. They were all fiberglass, flat-bottomed, specially made for the slow quiet business of stalking bonefish.

Grand stood looking down at the four empty berths, and the cut chains. He played with his beard, frowning. "Makes no sense," he said. "Why steal boats no good for anything but fishing on the flats—boats anyone can recognize?"

"For the motors?" Will said. "Batteries?"

"Then why not just take those?" He shook his head, and glanced up at us. "Anyone hear any noises last night?"

But we hadn't, and when they asked us the same question at the police station, later, we had nothing helpful to say. Constable Morgan wasn't on duty; there was another policeman, who didn't know Grand. He wrote down all the details of the theft on a big pad, very carefully, but he didn't seem to think there was much anyone could do. Grand gave him the identification numbers of the boats' motors, and even a photograph of one of the boats.

"You got insurance, of course," the policeman said.

"Thousand-dollar deductible," Grand said. "Whoever did this is costing me four thousand minimum."

The policeman whistled between his front teeth. "You got any personal idea who might have done it?"

Lou, beside me, started making an agitated humming sound like a kettle beginning to boil.

But Grand didn't say anything, and I couldn't bear it. I started to say, "It's the people who—" and Grand kicked me. The policeman didn't notice me or the kick; he couldn't see me over his high countertop.

"Thank you for the report, Mr. Peel," he said. "We'll do what we can. Let us know if you find any of the boats."

Outside the police station I said indignantly, "You *know* who stole them, it's the people who want to shut you up, the people who wrecked the farm!"

"Did you see them, Trey?" Grand said. "Can you prove it?"

"No, but—"

"Let's go see Grammie," he said.

We walked to the bank in the baking sunshine, down the dusty road. It's very hot in our islands in July, and there were hardly any people about, only a few chickens. The man who sells dollar bags of peanuts to tourists was propped against the wall of the market in the shade, asleep. Inside the door of the bank, the air-conditioning made the air wonderfully cool; it was like walking into a cold shower.

I love seeing Grammie behind the tellers' counter at the bank, looking all dressed up and dignified. She's a different person, there; she smiles at us quietly, and it's the other teller ladies who make a fuss of us. Or of Lou, really, because he's still young enough to be thought cute, though I can imagine what he'd say about that if he could talk.

Grand was cashing a check, and Lou was being clucked at by the ladies, when I saw Mr. Abbott the bank manager coming out of his office, looking solemn and businesslike. With him were two of the men I'd seen on Long Pond Cay, the ones I thought were French. The men who wanted to turn it into Sapphire Island Resort.

Lou turned his head, the way he so often does when he senses something in my mind. He saw them too, and at once his eyes went wide and he began to gasp, in that scary rhythmic pattern that can be the start of one of his seizures. Mr. Abbott and the two men glanced across, hearing him, and the taller of the two men caught sight of Grand, and paused. He stared at him for a moment, and stepped forward.

"Mr. James Peel," he said, in his accented English. "Our adversary, I believe."

"Good day, James," said Mr. Abbott nervously.

Lou was hooting and gasping, and I dragged him toward the door.

Grand nodded at Mr. Abbott, smiling. Then he looked at the Frenchman, and his smile dropped away. "Good morning," he said.

The tall man was wearing dark slacks, and a floppy white shirt that looked silky and expensive. He said easily, "I am Pierre Gasperi, and I am so sorry you do not approve of us. Mr. Abbott here will tell you that we are very sound people, financially. We shall be good for these islands, Mr. Peel."

"No, you will not," said Grand.

Mr. Gasperi's voice rose a little. "We are a force of nature, my friend."

Grand said, "No. Nature is a force against you."

Mr. Gasperi took a pair of dark glasses from his shirt pocket and put them on, as if he were setting a barrier between himself and Grand. He said softly, "If you are a wise man, you will change your mind."

And I don't know what Grand said to that, because Lou was making such a racket that I had to open the door and take him outside. He was better, once he was away from the Sapphire Island people.

I've never forgotten Mr. Pierre Gasperi's voice. It was very quiet and gentle, and really scary.

Grand said hardly anything all the way home, and when we got back he stopped the truck at the jetty, to look again at the cut chains of the lost boats. Lou jumped down and ran to our dinghy. He looked back at me and made his soft hooting sound. It was very clear what he wanted.

I said, "Grand, can we go out in the boat for a while?"

Grand glanced automatically at the sky, at his watch, and at the level of the tide. He said, "You got water in the boat?"

"Yes."

"Okay then. Back before dark." He gave me a small tight smile. "If you find a bonefish boat, bring it home."

But we saw no sign of the four missing boats, though we were both looking out for them. The water was very low, and all the white sandy shoals in the cut were exposed, with channels running between them. Even in our tiny dinghy it was easy to find yourself stuck, and I had to keep clear of our usual landing-place. It was a relief to be back at Long Pond Cay, after the things that had been happening.

I hadn't talked to Lou at all about the Otherworld. In a way, there wasn't much point. Not just because he can't talk, but because there was nothing to say. We both knew what had happened; we both knew nobody would believe it. And we both knew it would happen again. Now that we were really truly on our own, in a way we could be only in the boat, I said, as I watched for the channel, "Lou?"

He was sitting in the bow, holding the anchor-line. He looked back at me over his shoulder.

"Lou, did the tree really talk to you? Did it tell you what to do?"

Lou shifted round a bit and looked at me cautiously, even though I was the person he trusted most in the whole world. After a moment, he nodded.

I wished, for the millionth time in my life, that he could speak.

"Was it an accident, our going there?"

He shook his head firmly.

"Did they . . . call us?"

Lou nodded.

"D'you know why? D'you know what they want?"

Cautiously still, he made an oddly grown-up side-to-side movement with one hand: the gesture that means "sort of, a little bit, so-so."

I shook my head helplessly. "There's no way you can tell me, is there?"

Lou tried. He pointed ahead, at Long Pond Cay, with his eyes fixed on me to make sure I was watching. Then he pointed up at the sky, his arm stiff, straight up, pointing as high as he could. Then, because I still looked baffled, he reached out and gave me a little reassuring pat on the leg, and he grinned. It was such an open, happy, infectious grin that all the worry went out of me, and I laughed. It was as if our ages were suddenly reversed, and I was the little one and Lou the big kid.

We puttered up through the deeper blue-green water to the far end of the broad curving beach, and came inshore there, where an old buttonwood tree groped its branches out over the sand.

When the boat was anchored right we went up across the powdery white sand of the beach. It was littered with the leavings of the tide: pieces of purple sea fan, bits of wood and broken sponge, and scraps of hairy rope, colored turquoise and a very bright blue. Casuarina needles lay in scribbles on the sand.

Lou ran ahead of me, inland, toward the lagoon, and I followed him through the tall stringy grass, between hard black patches of marl, and fleshy-leaved clumps of scrub set with little yellow daisy-like flowers. Over on the smooth sand near the lagoon there were hundreds of the faint star-shaped patterns that the little ghost crabs leave, when they dart in and out of their holes. It was quiet, quiet, with only the small distant splash of a fish jumping somewhere in the lagoon, and the cheeping of tiny birds in the casuarina pines.

But Lou was running ahead of me, the wet sand sucking at his sneakers, water rising up out of it to fill his footprints, and suddenly I realized what he had been wanting, why he had asked to come here now, at this particular moment. It was the time between tides again, when the sea had gone down and not yet started to come back. It was the time for crossing between the two worlds, and Lou wanted us to cross over. Perhaps he had heard the Otherworld calling him.

I saw him stop, head up, listening. Once more the air

was beginning to shimmer, and I could hear the breathing of the wind in the casuarina needles, even though no wind blew.

Lou flung his arms wide, welcoming, and the Otherworld rose before us again and took us in.

*　*　*

But there was a difference, this time.

We were in a kind of wasteland, a huge flat open place, and the air was filled with a distant growling hum. We stood on grass, but all around us was bare concrete, with a few small tufts of green sprouting bravely out of a crack here and there. The sky was a weird brownish color, lighter overhead, but dark and hazy near the horizon. Far away there were buildings of some sort, though the haze made it hard to see what they were.

Lou was looking all around him, puzzled, as if he had expected to find himself somewhere else. I stared all around too. I didn't know which way to go; we were miles away from anything. It was like being in the middle of a desert.

Then the noise in the background began to grow, very fast, into a deep snarl rising to a roar, and I saw lights coming toward us out of the haze. Closer, closer they came, and the roar grew louder, louder. We stood there staring, motionless as lizards, and over the flat land an enormous airplane came hurtling straight at us.

It was so fast and so huge that I knew we couldn't escape it; I was certain it was going to hit us. I grabbed

Lou, and we both dropped flat on the ground. Grass prickled my face; I pressed against the earth as if I could disappear into it. The noise was earsplitting, filling the world, swallowing us—and then at the last moment it changed, as the plane rose over us, climbing into the sky.

Lou let out his breath in a husky squeak, and we sat up and looked at each other—and laughed. It wasn't funny, goodness knows, but I suppose we were delighted to find ourselves still alive. I knew now that we must be on some vast airfield, but I still couldn't figure out where to go.

Before we'd really collected our wits, another plane came hurtling at us. This time we watched the lights growing as it came, and saw it rise into the air at the last moment, though we still ducked as it roared overhead. Lou tugged at my hand, his face screwed up with pain at the noise, and we scrambled up and ran over the grass, heading away, out of the airplanes' path. A third plane came thundering down the runway as we went; there must have been less than a minute between each of them.

Someone had seen us, even out there in the middle of nowhere. As we ran across the grass, another set of lights appeared ahead of us, smaller than the plane's, and a car was coming at us fast, with red and blue lamps flashing on its roof, and a high-pitched siren wailing. There wasn't much point in dodging; where could we go? I called to Lou and we stopped and stood there, waiting.

The car came so fast that it skidded sideways as it stopped. It wasn't really a car but an odd kind of van, with SECURITY written on it in big letters. The doors at its rear swung open and two people in dark red uniforms jumped out, a man and a woman. The man got to us first, glaring, and grabbed my arm.

"What the hell d' you think you're doing? How did you get out here?" He had thick eyebrows and a black mustache; they seemed to be bristling with anger.

The woman took Lou's hand; her voice was softer, but just as urgent. "Get in the van, quick, before you get killed!"

They hustled us up a step and into the back of the van. The doors swung shut, and the van started off again so abruptly that we half-fell sideways onto a bench along the side wall. It was like being in a little room. There were four small TV screens, high up, two in each side wall, and each of them showed a different picture, of planes or buildings or that same flat concrete desert. One of them showed a van with flashing lights, moving fast; perhaps it was the one we were in.

The man was muttering into a telephone. The woman stood looking down at us, swaying, clutching a bar set into the ceiling. "However did you get here?" she said. "Where did you come from?"

"We got lost," I said.

She didn't think much of that for an answer. She frowned, and looked at Lou.

"What's your name, little one?"

Lou gazed up at her, big-eyed.

"He's called Lou," I said. "He can hear you, but he doesn't talk. I'm Trey."

The van was moving really fast. There was a distant roar outside as another plane took off.

The woman said, "What do you mean, he doesn't talk? He's sulking?" She wasn't as fierce as the man, and she was quite young, with her hair pulled back in a pony-tail.

"He can't talk. He never has." I cut the words off as short as I could; I never like saying much about Lou, spe-cially when he's there to hear.

The man turned back from the telephone. "We're heading for the tower office," he said to the woman. He was very square and broad-shouldered; his muscled arms filled his sleeves to bursting. He scowled at me. "You try-ing to kill yourself, kid? How did you get over the fence?"

I said quickly, "There was a place with a hole." I didn't want gaps in the conversation, for them to have too much time to wonder about us. Lies were better than silence.

"What kind of hole?"

"A . . . a break. Looked as though something had smashed through. A car, maybe."

The woman was peering closely at Lou, her face softer, friendlier, almost worried. Her eyes were an inter-esting shape; I thought she might be Chinese, though I'd never seen a Chinese person except in pictures. "How can the boy never have talked? That can't be true, in this day and age. Which is your hospital region?"

I couldn't dream up an answer to that one. Luckily the van gave a great lurch and stopped, and the doors at the back swung open again, letting in a jumble of noise. They took us down the step, out of the van, and then we had to wait for a moment while a big tanker truck chugged by.

In that moment I looked up and saw the whole airport spread out before us, and it was awful. A dark haze hung over the place, turning the sky a yellowish brown, misting the outlines of everything I saw. Buildings were blurred on the horizon, and on the runways crisscrossing the airport, dozens of the immense planes crawled in lines, so far from us that they looked like fuzzy insects. Far away, you could see a blur of light rise or fall as a plane landed or took off. It was like a huge nightmare version of our little single-runway airport at home—but at home, the air was clear. Here, it was so thick with fumes and smoke that even taking a breath made me want to cough.

Then we were hustled in through two tall metal doors, into bright light and shiny white walls and a bustle of people. They were a mix of people, just like at home, assorted shapes and sizes and complexions, but there was something odd about them. They reminded me of a crowd of ants, rushing to and fro, pausing sometimes for an instant but never really making contact with each other. Nobody took much notice of us, as the square-shouldered man led us through; they all kept glancing instead at television screens set at intervals high on the walls. These weren't tiny security screens like the ones in the truck; they were huge, and they all seemed to be showing pictures of war.

Images were flicking by one after the other on those screens: streets full of tanks, airplanes streaking across the sky, buildings exploding and vanishing into clouds of smoke. A man desperately dragged a body across a street, and the body had lost a leg. There was a flash of an anguished face, with blood running down its cheek. Then a shot of two soldiers firing machine guns through an open door. Though all the images were violent, there was no sound at all. The ant-like crowds were watching a war that looked as if it was being conducted in silence.

Then we were pushed into a room where the screens were not just here and there, but all around the walls. There were long banks of screens, all bright and flickering, on three sides of the room; it made me dizzy to look at them. Lou stood still, staring, fascinated. Three men sat at control panels, one before each bank, and in the middle of the room another was getting out of his chair beside a big desk. He was very tall, and had a close-cropped black beard; he looked down at us.

"How did they get there?" he said to the woman with the ponytail.

"Through a hole in the fence, apparently."

He gestured at the screens. One whole bank of them seemed to have pictures of the airport. "There are no holes."

"We're having the perimeter checked," said the broad-shouldered man who'd brought us in.

The bearded man came close, and stared at us. He had a long scar on one cheek, that made a divide in that side of his beard.

"Just kids," the woman said.

"But in such oddly old-fashioned clothes." He was looking at my sneakers. I couldn't see his own shoes.

She said lightly, "Retro's always fashionable. You know how kids are."

He said to me suddenly, "Don't you know what danger you were in? You and your little friend?"

"My brother," I said automatically.

"That makes it the more stupid."

I thought suddenly that it might help if I tried to seem really stupid. I let my mouth gape open a little, and blinked at him foolishly.

"Please mister, we wanted to see the planes," I said.

"Where do you live?"

I gazed at him even more vacantly. "Wanted to see the planes," I said again.

The woman moved restlessly. She said, "Sir, they're just children. And not too bright—probably castoffs from the projects. I don't think you need bother with them. We'll get them some medical attention, put them in a home—the young one seems to be an interesting speech-loss case."

The man turned his staring eyes on Lou, who was still gazing at the screens. He reached out and tilted Lou's chin toward him; then turned his head from side to side. He said slowly, "I've seen this face before."

Lou smiled at him serenely, and shook his head.

The man turned and spoke briefly to a woman at one of the banks of screens; she pressed some buttons and in a few moments we were looking at two dozen images of a tree, seen from above, with a small figure next to it. The picture widened, and now there was a dark ring all round the tree; the figure turned to cross this ring, and the camera zoomed in on his face. It was Lou, crossing the ditch full of giant millipedes.

Voices murmured in the room.

The bearded man took hold of Lou by the shoulders; his face was tight and angry. He said, "Two of my men were killed trying to rescue you from the Wilderness that day, little boy. They died, and you disappeared. Now suddenly you come out of nowhere again. *What is going on?*"

He gave Lou a shake. Lou whimpered, and I could hear his breathing getting louder, on the way to the start of a seizure. I forgot about trying to seem stupid, and I jumped forward. "My brother can't talk," I said.

"Then you talk for him. Who sent you?"

He let go of Lou, but he looked even angrier; his

mouth was a mean straight line now. I knew he wouldn't believe me if I told the truth, but I didn't know what else I could do.

I said, "Nobody sent us. We just found ourselves here, for no reason. We come from a different world."

He shook his head impatiently. I'd been right. "Not too bright, huh?" he said to the woman with the pony-tail. "Bright enough to invent fairy-stories. These two are from the Underground."

EIGHT

I never did discover what he was, this man with the scar-divided beard. Some kind of Head of Security, I suppose—a top policeman. He had us taken to his own office, an amazing big room full of expensive-looking furniture. It was high up, with enormous windows overlooking the whole airport. The daylight was beginning to fade, and you could see lines of different colored lights crisscrossing out there, reaching into the distance. I'd never looked down from somewhere so high, except in the airplane going to Nassau.

The woman who'd picked us up from the runway came too. He called her Nora; she called him Sir. It obviously wasn't his name, but it's the only label I have. On the way in, she gave us each a sort of candy bar, and I wondered if it was safe for us to eat it, but Lou instantly bit into his, and the smell of it made me so hungry that I did the same. It tasted wonderful, like a mixture of mango and orange and chocolate.

"Wow!" I said, swallowing. "I wish we had this at home."

"Where's home?" Nora said casually.

I didn't know what to say to that. *Earth? The twenty-first century?* I said, "The islands."

"Sit down here," Sir said to me. His voice was quiet; he seemed to have put away his angriness. He pointed to a weird chair made of shiny metal, with black padding on the seat and back. I looked at it doubtfully; it was rather like the dentist's chair in our island clinic.

But suddenly Lou started making his happy sound, the excited series of little grunts that always makes everyone smile, and we all looked at him. He was hopping about in front of a wall filled with shelves and pictures. The pictures seemed to be photographs of trees and flowers and animals, and on the shelves a few brilliant objects were set here and there, each on its own, illuminated by a small intense beam of light. One of them looked like a gleaming white piece of brain coral, another a spray of blue flowers. A third, at which Lou was staring, was a tiny jeweled bird.

"Ooo, ooo," went Lou. He half-reached for it, then glanced up enquiringly at Sir.

For once, Sir's grim bearded face was relaxed, almost smiling. "All right," he said. "You can pick it up."

Lou reached out, and I came over to see. There on his palm was a little copy of a hummingbird, painted in bright enamels, set with jewels, wonderfully done. It was really beautiful, except of course that it wasn't real.

Nora was looking over my shoulder. "Exquisite," she said.

Sir said, "Beauty is transient." His voice was much softer, less rasping. "I make a point of paying tribute to the extinct species."

Extinct. I looked back at the hummingbird, then round the walls at the pictures. I saw an eagle, a tiger, a leopard, a rhinoceros; lots of brilliantly colored fish, a sequence of small birds, a beautiful little frog. *Extinct.*

Lou put the enameled bird back in its place. He'd stopped making his happy sound.

"Sit down," Sir said to me again, and he moved me to that sinister chair. "Don't be afraid. Nobody's going to hurt you."

I was frightened all the same. I could feel my hands shaking, and I felt sick. I sat down on the chair, and Nora came closer. She smiled at me.

"It's all right, Trey," she said.

Then she put a strap over each of my arms, not tight, just enough to keep it against the arm of the chair, and another across my chest. And Sir put a kind of metal circle on my head, round my forehead. It rested there lightly. It felt cold.

He said, "That's it. All I want is to ask you a few questions. Who do you live with, you and your little brother?"

"Our grandparents," I said.

I heard Lou give an odd little gasp, and when I turned my head, I saw him staring at a broad flat screen that filled part of the wall opposite the pictures and shelves. It was like a huge television screen; I hadn't noticed it before. On the screen I saw Grand and Grammie, in their kitchen: Grand at the table with some papers, Grammie at the stove. They were very fuzzy, and they moved very slowly as if they were underwater, but it was definitely them. As I looked, they flickered and were gone.

Sir said softly, "And where is that?"

"Lucaya, in the Bahamas," I said. And there on the screen was our island, just as it flashed into my mind: green casuarinas and silver-top palms, white beach, blue-green sea. It was fuzzy again, but beautiful. Again, in the instant that I looked, it was gone.

"Very remote," Sir said to Nora. "Extraordinary. Most places like that have been under the sea for decades."

She said, "They've brought them a long way."

Sir reached out and swung my chair round a little, so that the screen was just out of my view. He said casually, "Who first took you Underground, Trey?"

The answer to that was "Bryn" and there was no way I could keep it out of my mind. I said nothing, but I knew that this mind-reading machine, or whatever it was, must now be putting a fuzzy image of Bryn on the screen. Perhaps they wouldn't recognize him.

But they did. I heard Nora take a sharp breath. And Sir said softly, "Ah yes. Of course."

I tried hard to think just about Bryn, so that I wouldn't give them the faces of any of the others. I didn't know whether it worked; I couldn't see the screen.

Sir said, "Can you tell me where any of the entrances are?"

"No," I said truthfully.

He sighed. "No. They're too sharp for that. They just took you. How did they get you into the Wilderness?"

The last question was so quick and quiet that I knew my brain must be showing them the answer in a picture, so there was no point in hiding anything. "From under-neath," I said. "From a tunnel. It was full of water, fast water. They said someone was trying to drown them."

Sir gave a short, cold laugh. "They were right," he said. "And why had they brought you all that way from your little island? Why did they take you to the Wilderness?"

"It was just the nearest place, I guess," I said. "They were trying to escape from the water."

"Come now, young Trey," Sir said. There was a chilly edge to his voice. "They had reasons. We saw you, remember? And your brother, with that ditch of mutant creatures. *Why did they want you there?*"

I said, "I don't know."

Sir sighed. He leaned over and turned my chair back, and with the other hand took the metal circlet off my head. As I caught sight of the screen again I saw the thick green undergrowth of the Wilderness, and the twisted, ancient tree in the clearing—and then they were gone. Nora pulled the straps off my arms and chest, and as she did, I saw tiny gleaming pads of metal on the underside of the fabric.

"That will do," Sir said. He looked over at Lou and patted the seat of the chair. "Come here, small one. Your turn."

Lou stood still, gazing at him, and my heart sank. If they tried strapping him on that chair, he'd start gasping and grunting and go into a seizure; he didn't mind children, but he hated being touched by any strange adult. Grammie hadn't yet been able to get him to go to school; it was the main reason why he couldn't yet read or write, though we were all trying to teach him.

I said quickly to Sir, "Please don't—he just can't do that. He's not like . . ."

But my voice trailed away, because Lou was already trotting over to the chair, hoisting himself up into it. Sir gave him a helpful boost. I stood there gaping. Lou caught my eye, and grinned, as they put the bands over his arms and chest, and the metal circlet on his forehead. Nora had to shorten that, to keep it from dropping down onto his nose.

Then Sir began talking to him, and very soon I understood why Lou was so unconcerned. Always I kept forgetting, here in this Otherworld, that although I was still the same person I'd always been, my little brother was different. A hundred miles different, a whole world different. I hadn't the remotest idea of the things that he could do, here.

Sir said, quiet and friendly, "Are you homesick, Lou?"

Lou cocked his head to one side and then shook it, no. I looked at the screen. It was blank.

"Are you hungry?"

Lou promptly nodded, and on the screen there was a fuzzy image of the candy bar Nora had given each of us. We all laughed.

"Those black creatures in the Wilderness," Sir said, in the same calm voice, "why weren't you afraid of them?"

Lou smiled at him, but on the screen there was nothing but lines of crackling static, the way a TV set looks when the programs are all done.

Sir took a quick breath, and paused for a moment. "I see," he said slowly. Then he said, "They killed two of my men, Lou—how come they didn't hurt you?"

The screen was still crackling and blank, and Lou turned his head to peer at it. He looked curious, as if he was checking to see whether it would show anything.

Nora checked the straps on Lou's body, and the metal circle round his head, but the screen didn't change. "There's nothing wrong, " she said.

"No. Once in a great while, it meets its match," Sir said. "This is pointless—take those things off him." He stood looking down thoughtfully at Lou for a moment while Nora disconnected him. He said, almost to himself, "You're the one they want, aren't you? Something happened to you in the Wilderness. Something they've been waiting for. We just have to find out what it is."

Then he glanced over at me again. "Where did they take you, after my men died?" he said. "Back down the tunnel?"

I said, "I don't suppose you'll believe me, but we were back where we came from, in the very next second."

Maybe he did believe me. He stood there looking into space, rubbing one forefinger up and down his cheek. Then he moved to a panel under the big screen and pressed some buttons. "For your interest," he said, "here is the Wilderness as the Underground left it that day."

The picture that filled the screen must have been taken from one of those helicopters. We were high up, looking down at a blackened, lumpy landscape from which the tall, burned stumps of trees jutted upward like black spines. Here and there a curl of smoke rose into the air. We moved to one side, then the other, then rose higher. All around, there was nothing but cinders and ash. The Wilderness had been burned into nothing. Of the lush green growth we had seen the last time, all that remained was a black desert.

"The fire my men had set was contained," Sir said, "but your friends from the Underground set more fires as they ran. They were prearranged, those fires. They burned very fiercely, and the wind carried the flames to our research facility, deep in the woods. A very valuable place, where we did vital work on genetic mutation. When that caught fire, there were huge explosions that must also have been preset. They were all ready to destroy the Wilderness, they were just waiting. Waiting for whatever it was that had happened, that day."

He squatted on his heels beside Lou so that he could

look him in the face. His skin was fairly dark, and the scar that ran into his beard stood out, in a nubbly white line. He glanced up at me too, and he said, quiet but fierce, "They are fanatics, do you understand that? Fanatics. Their only aim is destruction, of all the glories of our civilization. We have vanquished every major disease, we have found ways to feed and house every being on this planet, we have learned to resist the changes in climate as they come. Human kind has finally achieved control of life on Pangaia. But the fanatics of the Underground can see none of this. They fight their Greenwar to bring down the global government and substitute anarchy. They're mad, of course. But very dangerous."

He stood up again, and put his hands under Lou's arms to lift him gently down from the chair. Then he took a little box out of his pocket and pressed a switch on it. It buzzed softly.

"And they brought you from your distant island for some dark connected purpose," he said. "Related I think to an ancient festival that used to take place a few days from now, on August first. Ignorant superstition, like all their talk. They have been threatening doom for that date over the webwork, threatening a sacrifice. The end of our world, and the beginning of another. Mad. Unless this law and that law are changed, they are threatening, they will do such things. . . ."

He looked at Nora in a helpless kind of way. "Can

you believe I am trying to explain this to a pair of children?" he said.

"Why not?" she said. "One of them is . . . unusual."

Lou was trotting round the room again, gazing up at the pictures. He reached out once more to touch the jeweled hummingbird, but paused at the last moment, and drew back his hand.

Sir gripped my shoulder, hard. I glanced up and saw the black eyes staring down at me, still fierce. He said, "Your brother has a talent that they need, and might kill for. Be warned, work with the Government, and we will keep you both safe."

Before I could give that the smallest thought, the door opened and several people came hurrying in, men and women, all in the same sleek dark red uniform as Nora. Sir looked at one of them, a small thin man with sharp eyes and a completely bald head. "I want these two taken to Central, to be examined by Dr. Owen and Dr. Karminsky," he said. "They will have been informed. Keep them there overnight, and then bring them back here."

He looked me in the eye again. "Don't worry," he said.

The small bald man nodded at me encouragingly, but it didn't stop me worrying. I didn't like the idea of being "kept safe" by the Government one bit. The whole group of police took us outside.

We never saw Sir again.

Along gleaming corridors they took us, past more of those war-filled screens, and then into a wide elevator with metal walls. I saw Lou's eyes widen as the doors of the elevator swung silently together, and he felt the pressure of the rising floor under his feet. It was his first time in an elevator. He's never been to Nassau, he's never left our island, and though he's seen life in the rest of the world on television, there's a lot he hasn't seen or done.

In the Otherworld there was a lot that I hadn't seen or done either. The elevator doors hissed open and we were out on the top of the building, at the edge of a wide flat roof, with the airport's crisscrossing lines of lights spread all round us and a thick brown haze above, merging into darkness. You could see a star here or there in the sky, but very few, and none that I could recognize. We both know the stars, Lou and I; it's one of the things Grand's hot on. He says anyone who lives among islands and boats should know how to navigate by the stars. Looking at the darkness, I wondered suddenly whether it was night in our own world, whether Grand and Grammie would be frantic because we weren't back home. Somehow I didn't think so. Time in the Otherworld didn't match the way time passed at home.

The air filled with noise; a helicopter was hovering above us, coming down very slowly toward the roof. Its door opened as it touched down, and we were shoved inside, hands forcing our heads down so they wouldn't be chopped off by the rotors. The shape and size of the rotors looked quite different from the ones I'd seen in our world, but I couldn't figure out how.

EIGHT

Two men got in with us, and put Lou and me together in a seat at the back, and up we went, fast. Lou was next to the window, looking down, making soft little amazed noises. He glanced up at me, and grinned. I couldn't help grinning back, though I can't say I felt much like it. Looking out from up there, we must have been able to see for miles. And everywhere we looked, in every direction, there were lights: chains and necklaces of lights, moving strands of light that must have been roads, endless dots of light. Endless people.

First I thought how beautiful the lights were, but in the next instant I realized they showed how incredibly crowded this place must be. It was like the phosphorescence in the sea that Grand showed us sometimes after dark, at home; when you stirred up the seawater, it glowed like liquid fire—but the light didn't come from the water itself. It came from all the thousands and millions of tiny glowing creatures swarming in every inch.

The helicopter was very noisy. Nobody spoke to us. Sir and Nora had treated us like people, but now we were just objects, to be shuttled around. The only trouble was, I didn't know where we were being shuttled to. What was Central? A hospital? "We'll keep you safe" could have meant anything, even some sort of prison.

We flew for quite a long time, half an hour maybe, and Lou fell asleep, his head drooping against my shoulder. It was amazing how he could just tune everything out. Still, he's young. It made me feel lonely. I sat there with my mind worrying away a mile a minute, staring out at those endless dots and strings of light, that went on and on without a break anywhere.

When we did come down, it was into a place really thick with lights, and as we slowly dropped closer and closer to the ground I looked out of the window and saw dozens of great tall buildings reaching up to meet us, sky-scrapers I guess, all of them blazing with light. On the other side I saw only darkness, a broad strip of darkness before the sea of lights began again, hazy in the distance. When the helicopter touched down, with a gentle jolt, I realized that this darkness was a river, and that we were landing on a flat place where the river and the city met. Floodlights shone down over the landing area, and at its edge you could see the river lapping against a barrier wall. In the light, the water was a dark grey-brown.

Still nobody spoke to us. They took us across a paved space and onto a moving staircase that rose steeply upward. Lou loved it, he chortled with surprised delight as it carried him up. People climbed past us even while we moved; the place was crowded and busy and every-one seemed to be in a hurry. Pangaia was a world I could never have imagined, from what I knew at home. Every-where we had been, the land was paved or concreted and built over, jammed with people. The air was hazy and the water was brown, and no stars shone. Only the weird mutated Wilderness had been green, and now that was black and dead. It was all about as different from Lucaya as any place could be.

We stepped off the staircase, with a silent man in uniform at either side of us. This place did look as if it might be a hospital; it was all glass and steel and white paint, with long bleak corridors, and plateglass doors that slid open when you walked toward them. Men and women in white coats or white overalls hurried about the corridors, murmuring to each other, each carrying a little flickering screen the size of a book. Everyone looked worried; nobody smiled.

Our two red-uniformed guardians marched us along miles of gleaming corridor and delivered us at last to an airy room filled with strange-looking computer equipment, all wires and screens and banks of levers and buttons. We found ourselves facing a small bald man with bright blue eyes and a nut-brown face. He wore a long white coat and white shoes, and he was sitting on a stool gazing at us both with great interest. He had one of those book-sized screen things in his hand. He was so obviously expecting us that when the two silent uniformed men brought us in, he just nodded at them and waved them away. And they saluted and went.

There was nobody else in the room. Some of the equipment was humming softly. The man's face was creased and friendly, and as our guards left, he got to his feet and held out a hand for me to shake. I took it with a firm grip, and got one back. Grand was very big on firm handshakes, he told us they were a test of character.

"You're Trey and Lou," said the nut-brown man, and he shook Lou's hand too. "I'm Dr. Owen, and I have to take some measurements. Don't worry. Nothing to scare you. Stand here—look."

There were two round raised discs in the middle of the room, and he went over and stood on one of them. He beckoned to me, and pointed to the other. I hesitated.

Dr. Owen grinned at me. "Ah come on, Trey," he said. "Have faith. I guarantee you everything's harmless in here."

Cautiously, I crossed over and stepped up onto the disc. It was a little raised platform, about a foot high.

Dr. Owen whistled. It was a quick little two-tone whistle, the way you'd call a dog.

There was a whirring sound, and a squat, square box came trundling toward me over the floor. It moved like that chunky round robot in the first *Star Wars* movie, if you remember him, but that was about the only likeness. It wasn't cute and it didn't have flashing lights or make squeaky gurgling noises; it was dead quiet and rather sinister. While I stood there, nervously watching, it moved slowly round me, and I noticed there were half a dozen upright wires sticking up from its top like aerials, each with a glowing light on the end. The lights swiveled sometimes, and flickered.

Dr. Owen beckoned to Lou, and stepped off his round

platform, and without even being told, Lou trotted cheerfully over toward him and hopped up onto it. I was baffled again by the way so few things in Pangaia seemed to frighten him; it was as if he knew what to expect.

The moving box finished circling me, and trundled over toward Lou.

"This is Fred," said Dr. Owen. "Fred sees all. Though not inside your head, you'll be happy to know. Here's what he made of you, Trey."

He pressed a few buttons on the book-sized thing he had in his hand, and in a wide metal cabinet against one wall, a big screen lit up. Pangaia seemed to be full of screens, as if nobody there wrote words down on paper, as if everyone thought only through pictures.

On the screen, I saw a larger than life image of myself, a spooky hollow 3-D image drawn in thousands of intertwining lines. It moved slowly around. Then it vanished, and was replaced by columns and columns of numbers, flicking down, over and over, a new screenful every second.

"Vital statistics," Dr. Owen said. "You're a toy, to Fred. He's figured out how you work. He could replicate you—you wouldn't have a mind, but you'd be a perfect clone otherwise." He peered more closely at the screen for a while, studying the numbers, and his voice changed. "I must say," he said more slowly, "you are an interestingly obsolete model, Trey."

Fred was making his way round Lou, his antennae

standing up like stiff hairs. When he had finished, Dr. Owen put Lou's strange interwoven image on the screen in place of mine. He gazed at it for a long time, playing with the buttons on his hand keyboard to move it about in different directions. Then he switched it off, sat down on his stool again, and faced us.

He looked me in the eyes, his face serious and intent. "Where do you come from?" he said.

Perhaps it was the handshake that made me trust him.

"Not from Pangaia," I said.

"No indeed," said Dr. Owen. He was studying Lou now, and smiling a little, an amazed sort of smile. Lou smiled back. He stepped off the round platform, and sat down on its edge next to Fred.

"Possibly from Pangaia long ago," Dr. Owen said quietly, almost to himself. "Possibly from some wholly other . . . place. But no, not from Pangaia."

"The other man didn't believe me," I said.

"What other man?"

"They just called him Sir."

Dr. Owen laughed abruptly. "I'll bet they did," he said. "We all call him Sir. No—he didn't believe you, he thinks you are a product of the Underground."

"Do you think we are?" I said.

"Of course not," said Dr. Owen.

I said suddenly, just as it came into my head, "What do you think of the Underground?"

Dr. Owen sat there expressionless on his stool for a

moment, as if he were trying to figure out what to say. I think he was one of those people like Grand, who take kids just as seriously as they do grown-ups.

He said at last, "I am a neuroscientist, Trey. A kind of doctor. I'm in the business of observing and preserving human life. So my occupation puts me on a different wavelength from the Underground. They don't have a high opinion of *Homo sapiens*, those folks—they think we've ruined our planet."

"But what do they want to *do*?" I said. I glanced at Lou, but he didn't seem interested in this at all; he was sitting next to Fred, running a finger gently up and down one of his spiky antennae.

"Nobody knows," Dr. Owen said. He sighed. "Perhaps they want to give us back our soul, our global conscience. But we lost that long ago."

He lifted the book-sized keyboard thing to his mouth, and spoke to it. "Escort to RE Six," he said.

I said uneasily, "What's RE Six?"

"Forgive me for this, Trey," he said, although he didn't move a muscle. Fred made a faint clicking sound, and a kind of lever shot out from the side of his square body and touched Lou's upper arm. Then it was gone again.

Lou looked down at his arm in surprise, and then gently keeled over sideways, so that he was lying on one side on the round platform. I shouted in fright and ran to him, but he didn't seem hurt. He blinked at me, looking puzzled.

Dr. Owen said quickly, soothingly, "A muscle relaxant only, I promise you. It will wear off in half an hour. Some people very senior to your friend Sir have ordered a special psychological scan on your little brother, a scan that is harmless only if the subject is not tense."

"You can't *scan* him!" I said in panic. "He's only a little boy!"

Dr. Owen spread his hands. "Not my territory, Trey," he said. "I deal with the body. What they want is to see inside his mind."

The door opened, and two men in green overalls came in. One was young, broad-shouldered, the other one older, with short grey hair. They were pushing a kind of trolley, like a hospital gurney, with a sheet on top. Without a word they picked up Lou and laid him on his back on the sheet. He didn't make a sound, and he didn't move.

I said, "I'm going too!" I heard my voice squeak, I was so frightened.

"Of course," said Dr. Owen. He put a hand on my shoulder. "So am I. It's not far—a test facility two floors up."

The two men headed out of the door pushing Lou, and I followed with Dr. Owen. They walked fast along the glowing white corridor, which was completely bare except for little moving machines high upon the wall at each corner. Perhaps they were cameras, watching us. The men raced round a corner—and then suddenly skidded the trolley to a stop and swung round so fast I could hardly tell what happened. The younger one lunged at Dr. Owen, seized the little screen out of his hand and pressed it against the side of his head. There was a tiny muffled thud, and Dr. Owen fell to the floor without a sound.

The man grabbed my arm, the other one picked Lou up under his arm as if he were a parcel, and we ran down the corridor to a door with a red light over it. They pulled the door open.

I looked back. I'd rather liked Dr. Owen.

The younger man said urgently in my ear: "We're taking you to Bryn. Get down, now!" He pushed me down so I was crouching. "Curl up in a ball, arms round your knees," he said, and he pushed me out of the door.

NINE

found myself sliding down some kind of chute, very steep, very dark, with a sour smell. It swung sideways, and then I fell in a heap, out in light again, floundering in a pile of sheets and clothes. The others came tumbling down after me. An empty sleeve flapped round my neck; I saw Lou lying on his back in a white nest like an unmade bed. We had come down a laundry chute; we were all in a great heap of dirty laundry. If I hadn't been so scared, I would have laughed.

And then the men were tugging us out, the older one with Lou under his arm again, and we were outside a door and in cooler air, on a dark street.

It was a narrow street with uneven paving, like round stones set into dirt. The men hurried us down it and turned into a side alley, and then another; it was so dark, I don't know how they knew where they were going. The alleyways seemed to run between tall stone buildings with no windows, like a black maze. This was totally different from anywhere else we'd been in Pangaia.

Then we were out again in a wider street lit by the occasional dim lamp, and through a brown haze you could see battered doors and unlighted windows, some of them broken. The men paused at an entryway with two huge closed wooden doors, and pushed open a smaller door set into one of them. We stepped up and over, and found ourselves in a kind of courtyard, with the dark sky overhead and a blur of voices from all around. It was like a hollow apartment building. On both sides of the court-yard, iron stairways went up to a balcony, and then again to another balcony above that, and the doors of the apartments led off the balconies, three on each side of the square. The walls were scarred and peeling, the iron rusted. This building wasn't in good shape.

We clattered up a stairway and past open doors on the first balcony. A spicy smell of cooking came from one of them, and another must have been a toilet, and smelled terrible. There were holes in the floor, here and there, though not big enough to fall through.

A woman's voice called softly from a lighted window, "A rescue, Steven?"

Our older man called back, "A rescue!" in a kind of loud whisper, and the woman clapped her hands.

Then we went through a door and a stuffy carpeted entryway, and into a room filled with light and people, all sitting round a table, and at the head of the table was Annie, smiling like sunup, with the girl Gwen sitting beside her.

They gave us such a welcome, it was as if we'd come

back from the dead. They'd been eating, and they gave us bread and cheese and fruit—apples and cherries, things that don't grow on Lucaya—and a sort of spicy chocolatey drink. Gwen made room for me next to her, with Lou on my other side next to Annie. He seemed to be getting movement back in his arms and legs now, gradually. The man who'd been carrying him propped him in his chair, and Lou leaned his head against Annie trustingly. She put her arm round him. It was almost as if he'd come home.

There were seven or eight men and women round the table, a mixture of ages, all of them sort of scruffy-looking, with shaggy hair and clothes that looked home-made and didn't quite fit. They were all important people in the Underground, we found out, and the only reason they were here above ground, in hiding, was because they'd been looking for Lou and me.

"When the worlds touch," Annie said, "we know if you are here, but not where we shall find you. Gwen is our seer, she tells us where you are. And if the authorities have you, someone from the Underground will always be able to reach you, to carry you away. We are everywhere in their spoiled world, everywhere in their government, but they can't tell who we are, even with their wonderful technologies."

I glanced at Gwen, and she gave me her quick squinty-eyed grin. She didn't look like a seer, more like Marty Black, who sat behind me at school and was always in trouble for giggling.

Annie had me tell them everything that had happened

to us since we arrived, and they listened very intently. They exchanged looks once in a while, specially at the bit where Sir told me the Underground wanted Lou's talent and might kill for it. I paused, then.

"Is that true?" I said.

"Yes," Annie said. "We would kill, or we would die. But you knew that, didn't you?"

I suppose I did, after seeing what happened to the Wilderness.

When I'd finished, Annie said, "We have very little time left now. They will be looking for you everywhere." She took a deep breath, and turned her head to me. "Trey—I told you your brother was prophesied, in Pangaia. That we were waiting for him. Now we should tell you why. This is the prophecy all of us in the Underground learned when we were children, from our parents and our parents' parents and who knows how many generations before that."

She looked round the room, and she said in a loud, firm voice, "For love of life, Gaia sends Lou."

"Silent as stone," said the old man on her left.

A redheaded young woman beside him said, "The tree speaks to him. He walks through stars."

"Out of the labyrinth. The weaver spins him," said a dark, narrow-faced man next to her, and I saw that it was Math.

"Into rebirth," said his neighbor, a heavyset, grey-haired woman.

"Towering green," said the next man, younger and fair-haired, with pockmarked skin. "At Loonassa."

The man beside him had a hesitation in his speech. He said, "T-to save P-Pangaia."

"For love of life," said Gwen quietly, beside me. She saw the baffled look on my face, and reached to the center of the table for a thin, leather-covered book. She opened it. "Look, then, Trey," she said.

I looked at the neat handwriting on the page.

> "For love of life
> Gaia sends Lugh
> Silent as stone.
> The tree speaks to him
> He walks through stars
> Out of the labyrinth
> The weaver spins him
> Into rebirth
> Towering green
> At Lughnasa
> To save Pangaia
> For love of life."

I looked up from the page and found myself facing Lou. He sat there unconcerned, smiling a little, and I suddenly felt he had known these peculiar words all his short life.

I looked back at the page. I said stupidly, "The spellings are different."

"The sound of the words is the same," Gwen said. "Lou is Lugh."

"But what does it mean?"

"Lou knows," Annie said. "Don't you, Lou?" Her white hair was in a rough knot at the back of her head, her elegant chin held high; she looked like a raggle-taggle queen.

Still smiling his half-smile, Lou reached to the plate of fruit on the table and held up half an apple to me.

Annie laughed. "All right. Lou knows half of it."

I was getting cross. "But I have to know too!"

"Of course you do," she said at once, and reached over to pat my arm. "Trey—those words are very old. They are carved into a wall deep down at the start of the labyrinth, the maze of old tunnels under the deepest part of the city, which has been there for centuries. Deeper even than we live. Underneath the Underground. Gaia, the central force of our world, she put those words there." Her dark eyes were looking straight into mine, and I felt the hairs prickle on the back of my neck.

She said, "We who are the children of Gaia know that those words are there for a crisis, and that the crisis is now. They tell Lou to go into the labyrinth, to accomplish there whatever the tree has told him to do, and thus to achieve the rebirth of Pangaia. He must do this, and he knows it. It is why he chose to come here."

It was true that Lou was the one who'd brought us

here this time, by urging me to go to Long Pond Cay at the moment the worlds touched, between tides.

"But I'm going with him," I said. "Wherever he goes."

They all nodded, and there was a murmur of agreement round the table.

Lou took my hand.

Math said, "We have a saying here: *my brother saves me so that I may save him.*"

"I'd come too, if they'd let me," Gwen said. She would have done too, I think; she was a tough little thing.

Annie said, "Bryn will be here soon—he is the door-keeper of the labyrinth. He has gone to make sure we can pass back to the Underground in safety. Up here, everyone will be looking for you now."

"But not in these streets," said the old man beside her. He had a lined brown face and white hair; he looked a bit like Grand, without the beard. He grinned at me. "This is the underbelly of Pangaia, where the poor live," he said. "The people whom our wonderful civilization does not reach. The forgotten millions, who cling to life by their fingertips—and believe in the Underground."

The older of the two men who had brought us stuck his head into the room, and I realized they must have been keeping watch at the door. "Bryn is here," he said.

And big golden-bearded Bryn came in, scarcely recognizable in a ragged black jacket, with a greasy woolen cap pulled half over his face. He winked at Lou and me as if he had last seen us only five minutes before, and he didn't even say hello.

"Time," he said to Annie. "To the station, and through the service tunnel. The patrol comes back in twenty minutes. Time to go."

They were all on their feet so fast, they nearly knocked over the table. The redheaded girl stayed behind, but the others took us out through the courtyard and into the dark street, to a fenced stairway that led down under the ground. There were far more people down there than on the surface.

It was a subway, they said, an underground railway. I've never seen one in our own world, so I don't know if it looked the same. We went down long moving staircases into a big open space where men and women were hurrying to and fro. The people from the Underground stayed close round Lou and me so that nobody would notice us. But this crowd was made of busy, ordinary people who paid us no attention. They were rushing in and out of a wide set of about ten gates, and the underground trains were beyond that; you could hear a distant rumbling. We never saw the trains, though. Before we reached the gates, Bryn paused by the wall, outside a tall metal door with no handle, marked NO ENTRANCE. He tapped gently. The door swung slowly open and then back again, and before it was shut, five of us had slipped inside. Bryn, Annie, Gwen, Lou and me.

I never knew what happened to the others.

And I don't remember much of the whirl through underground pipes and tunnels, on those strange little trolleys of theirs that took us to the entrance to the labyrinth. In the dimlit dark, they knew where they were going, and we were simply carried along with them. It took a long time.

We came, at last, to a place where the tunnels were not round and man-made, or carved out by machines, but rough, rocky cave-tunnels, made over centuries by the stirring of the planet itself. There was no light of any kind here except the flickering glow from old-fashioned lanterns that we were all carrying. We came to a flat rock wall where Bryn, Annie and Gwen all stood still for a moment, and bent their heads. Then they held their lanterns close to the rock and showed us the lines that they had spoken to us earlier, the lines about Lou. My Lou, their Lugh.

You could only just make out the words. They looked as if they had been carved into the rock centuries ago.

> For love of life
> Gaia sends Lugh . . .

It was a spooky place. There was no sound except our own voices and footsteps; if we stood still and silent, you could hear only a slow drip of water somewhere deep in the cave, and once or twice a faint quick rustling sound. I didn't like the rustling; it made me think of rats. Shadows moved like dark ghosts all round us, as the lantern flames flickered.

Bryn said, his voice making a soft creepy echo, "This is the entrance to the labyrinth. There are two doors. The first I can open, the second can be opened only by Lou."

He gave his lantern to Gwen and stood facing the rock wall next to the carved words. Then he raised his hands high and put them on the wall, his fingers moving to and fro over it, looking for the feel of something. I couldn't see any sign of what it was, but in a few moments he must have found it, because a great creaking sound began, and he stood away from the wall.

A whole section of the rock moved inward a little, away from us, and then slid sideways, making a hideous screeching, scraping sound as it moved across. Inside, I could see only darkness. My throat felt very dry suddenly, and I could hardly swallow.

Lou came forward eagerly as if he were playing a game at school.

"Be careful!" I said, and my voice came out in a squeak.

He paid no attention. I don't think he even heard me. Holding his lantern as high as he could, he stepped through the black opening, and his light went with him and showed another cave, running into darkness on either side. It too was like a tunnel, and we were facing its side wall. We followed Lou in, and the light from all the lanterns together showed faint lines running up and across and down the wall, like the outline of another door.

Something was written in the rock of this door. Three words. Their letters were as old and worn as the others had been, and I had to trace them with my fingers before I could make them out. Then gradually I saw them, one by one.

> *Rigel*
> *Bellatrix*
> *Betelgeuse*

Annie said, "We have never known what these names mean."

"Only that they are the children of Gaia," Bryn said.

Lou grabbed my hand and tugged at it urgently, asking; he was too small to reach the words with his fingers, and he couldn't see them. With my eyes on his face, I read them out to him.

"Rigel. Bellatrix. Betelgeuse."

Lou stared at me for an instant, and then he gave his gurgling laugh-sound. I grinned back at him. For a moment I even forgot how scared I was. We both knew those three names. Grand had recited them to us often, rolling them off his tongue slowly as if he could taste them.

"You know them!" Gwen said. She clapped her palm against her fist, like a little girl. "Tell me!"

"They're stars," I said. "The brightest stars in Orion."
They all looked at me blankly.

"Orion. The constellation. The one that has three
stars in a row, for his belt. The belt of Orion. *You* know!"

But of course they didn't know. You could see Orion
from our world, not theirs. The air of their world was so
dirty, they could hardly see any stars at all.

I looked up at the names on the wall again—and
then I saw something else. Beside each name, there was a
round hole in the rock. Two of these holes were empty,
but in the third there was a little chunky, rocky star. I
knew just where I'd seen a star like that before.

"Bryn!"I said. "Look—next to the names!"

"Oh yes," Bryn said sombrely. "They are Gaia's great
mystery. The gaps have to be filled. Without them, Lou
can never open the door."

"Pick him up, please please, pick him up so he can
see!"

My voice was near a squeak again, I was so excited.

Bryn gave Gwen his lantern again, put his big hands
round Lou's waist, and hoisted him up. With one hand
Lou held his lantern close, with the other he ran his
small fingers over the little rocky star, the star that was
absolutely identical with the fossil star shell in his precious collection hidden on Long Pond Cay.

He beamed down at me, and made a happy little
honking sound.

Gwen said suddenly in a frightening, choked voice,

"Bryn! Put him down, quick! Trey, put down your lantern! Lou, you too!"

Startled, Bryn dropped Lou to the ground, and the two of us hastily put down our lanterns.

Gwen was showing the whites of her eyes the way Lou does in a seizure. Her body went rigid. Annie gave a dreadful desperate sound like a groan, and took her hand.

"The worlds are touching!" Gwen said in a strange, hoarse voice.

The lights of the lanterns began to swim in front of me, as if I were looking at them underwater. I felt Lou's hand take mine and hold on tight. I heard Bryn's voice calling, as if from a long way away.

"The stars! Find the stars!"

And the voice dwindled into the high song of the wind in the casuarina pines, and Lou and I were back in the sunshine, under the blue sky, on the long white beach of Long Pond Cay.

TEN

We both knew exactly where we wanted to go, of course. We turned and ran along the beach, on the firm white sand near the water, where your feet don't sink in. I can't tell you how good it was to be in the clear air and the cool sea breeze of the islands, after the dark tunnels of the Otherworld. After a minute or two, I pulled off my sneakers and splashed along in the shallows, just for the fresh cold feel of the seawater on my feet.

It was a long way to the other end of the bay, and our running slowed to a walk by the time we reached the low sandstone cliff, fringed with casuarinas, where the sea had carved out our little cave. Lou dived inside, and pulled back the chunk of rock that hid our special shells in their hole. He reached in, and held out his hand to me.

There it was: the little rock star, that had been a star shell once, before hundreds of thousands of years turned it into a fossil. It was exactly like the one set into the wall deep in the labyrinth. I whacked him on the back. "That's two of them, Lou!"

He put it carefully in the pocket of his shorts, and pulled back the rock to cover the others, but he shook his head in a worried way. He held up three fingers, and shrugged. He was right; neither of us had a clue where we might find a third stone star.

And then we saw something that knocked the stone stars right out of our minds. A few yards up the beach, where the scrubby undergrowth began, a tall flat notice board had been erected, on sturdy wooden posts. It was brand-new; the wood was still fresh and yellow. We ran round it, to see what was written on the other side.

In huge letters, the notice read, DANGER HEAVY MACHINERY AT WORK, and in smaller letters underneath, SAPPHIRE ISLAND RESORT.

* * *

We had been gone for no more than an hour of our own time; the notice was new. But when we went home and described it to Grammie and Grand, we found it was the end of a sequence of things that none of us had known about. Grand and his friends and all of us who cared for Long Pond Cay, we had lost our battle against Mr. Pierre Gasperi. During the weeks while the minister had put a temporary stop to development, he and his partners and their lawyers had managed to persuade Government that they would really bring good changes to the islands with their Sapphire Island Resort. They promised to employ local people, they printed elaborate studies about how many tourists they would attract to

Lucaya, and they rushed in experts from all over the world to explain how and why, in the long run, they would do no damage at all to the environment.

So Government, hoping to improve life on Lucaya, gave them permission to develop.

"And by the time people notice that the fish breeding grounds are gone, and the birds got nowhere to nest and feed," Grand said bitterly, "the damage will be good and done."

Things began happening much faster than they usually do in the islands. Before the developers began turning Long Pond Cay into Sapphire Island, they had to have somewhere on Lucaya to store their materials. They bought a big piece of scrubland at our end of the island, about half a mile from Grand's little marina, and they cut down all the trees and stripped the land until it was a big bare sandy parking area. It looked terrible.

Miles away in town, freighters came to the deepwater harbor and unloaded trucks and bulldozers and cranes and all kinds of heavy machinery, and after them loads and loads of concrete block and steel and cement and timber. Every day the big trucks thundered along our road from town, carrying it all to the parking ground. A big steel fence was put up there, all around the piles of supplies, with a gate and a security guard post.

Lou and I stood watching one day as the fence was being put up, with a crane hauling each section upright. He made his soft little hooting noise and nudged me, and holding his hand sideways like a fence he went one-two-three on the ground, showing three barriers. It was a moment before I realized what he was saying to me: *Look, that fence is like the ones we saw somewhere else. We're being turned into the Otherworld.*

An American voice yelled at us from the group of workmen near the crane. "Hey, you kids—get outta there!"

We weren't on his land, we were on our own island, but it didn't seem worth arguing.

I went to get the dinghy. I wanted to go to Long Pond Cay, even though Grand had told us he thought we should keep away, for fear of causing trouble. We hadn't been back since the day we rescued the fossil star shell, though we'd been looking in vain on every beach on Lucaya to find another one.

Lou trailed after me. He didn't seem enthusiastic. I couldn't understand him.

"Don't you want to look for the third shell?" I said. "That *must* be where we'll find it."

He shrugged. He got into the boat with me, but he wasn't hurrying. It baffled me; I thought he would be feeling a big sense of urgency—but then, he was the one who would know when we were called back to the Otherworld, not me. All I could do was wait. And after all, time in the Otherworld moves in a different way from the way time passes here. A second in one could be a month in the other, it seemed to me.

The developers had brought a huge dredge into the shallows round Long Pond from the open ocean. It made very slow progress because it had to dredge as it came, sucking up the sand, spitting it out into barges to be dumped on the parts of the island they wanted to build up. Gradually it dredged a channel through the flats, the shifting shoals where, once, only Grand and the bonefish guides and Lou and I had known how to find the way at low tide. Then it began to suck out the sand of the lagoon, the long pond that gave the cay its name.

Watching that dredge, I found myself with a hot feeling in my throat and tears in my eyes. Where would the bonefish go, now that their safe quiet tidal flats were being destroyed?

Grand said that bonefish were more intelligent than humans, and would very soon transfer themselves to other breeding grounds among the sandy uninhabited cays on the south side of Lucaya. He and his guides had new routes already, new favorite places where they could take the fishermen who loved to spend their holidays trying to catch a bonefish, fighting to bring it in, and then throwing it back to be free again. But nothing would make up for the loss of Long Pond Cay.

Big flat barges went to and fro over the shallows between Lucaya and the cay, taking machinery over to start moving the sand and rock around. The developers put up more of those tall notices on wooden legs at all the places where people used to land for picnics, as well

as the beach where Lou and I went. They still said DAN-
GER HEAVY MACHINERY AT WORK, and though
they didn't actually say KEEP OUT, that was the effect
they were meant to have.

The developers had no legal right to keep people off
the cay, Grand said, because the Government hadn't sold
them the island, but only let them lease it. Besides
which, he said, the land between high and low water-
marks anywhere in our country belongs to the people,
even on private islands. But those notices worked.
Tourists don't want to land on a beach for a peaceful pic-
nic and risk having to listen to bulldozers—specially
when they know there are plenty of other beaches on
other islands, with no sound but the wind and the sea.

And as for the local people—well, the first time that
Lou and I went ashore on Long Pond after more of the
notices went up, a man came yelling at us before we
could get halfway to our casuarina tree. He had a
machete in his hand; he was cutting brush, I guess. He
was Bahamian, but I didn't think he was from Lucaya. In
spite of all their talk about Lucayan jobs, the developers
had brought in a lot of workers from Nassau.

"Hey!" the man shouted. "You can't read? Get out of
here!"

I stood where I was, and glared at him. "We below
high-water mark," I yelled back. "This free land, you
can't throw us off!"

He came closer. He wasn't threatening us, but he was

scowling, and he did have that machete. "Danger notice mean danger," he said. "An' that mean if you get hurt here, ain't nobody's fault but yours. You don't want to make trouble for you families, right? Go play somewhere else, babies."

I took a deep breath, but Lou took my hand and pulled me back toward the boat. It was another of those times when he was the sensible one, and I was the little kid.

After that, we didn't go back to Long Pond Cay, even though it was our gateway to the Otherworld. When I lay in bed at night I would think of the Otherworld and wonder if we would ever get back there. Half of me hoped that we never would. As the months went by, it all seemed more and more like a dream, something I'd imagined, that had never really happened at all. It was only when I was alone with Lou, looking at those thoughtful dark eyes of his, that sometimes I would know with sudden awful certainty that the Otherworld was real, and that it was waiting for us.

But I wasn't alone with Lou much during schooltime. I got the bus to school in town every day, and he was going to the little local school now, where they had a new teacher, Miss Rolle, who seemed to know just how to cope with him. His reading was coming along pretty well, she said, though as Grammie pointed out, he wouldn't be able to show us that until he could write as well. He still got fussed under pressure, and of course he still didn't speak, but he hadn't had a seizure for a long time now.

Then something happened to change that.

I was coming out of school with my friend Kermit, both of us kicking a ball to and fro, when a car stopped in the street just in front of us. The ball was already on its way up from my foot, and it hit the car's side window. Didn't break it, but it made an impressive noise. The driver wound his window down.

"Sorry," I called. I grabbed up the ball from beside the car.

"Trey," said the man. "How you doin', Trey?"

I looked at him. He was a good-looking man, with a little fringe of a mustache, and he was wearing a short-sleeved white shirt. He grinned at me. There was a gold tooth shining at one side among all the white ones.

"I's your daddy," he said.

I stared at him. I didn't recognize him one bit, not that I ever could have done from that one blurry photograph.

"Uh," I said.

"How you doin'?" he said again.

"I'm fine," I said.

Kermit came close, his bright eyes curious. He's always a talker, bouncy, full of it. "You really Trey's daddy?" he said. "Wow!"

"Working on Sapphire Island," said my daddy, if that's who he was.

"Long Pond Cay," I said automatically.

He laughed. "You a chip off the old block, Trey baby. Sound like you grand-daddy. I heard about him and his campaign."

"Well," I said flatly. "It didn't work."

"Sure didn't. You look great, kid. You got so big! Hop in and I'll give you a ride home."

I fiddled with the ball. "I gettin' the bus," I said. "But thanks."

"This a nice car, man!" Kermit said, surveying it. "This your car?"

"Sapphire Island's car," my daddy said. He put it in gear again. He was still smiling, still good-tempered. "See you around, Trey. Have a good day."

And he drove off, a bit faster than necessary. We watched him go.

"Nice car you daddy got," Kermit said again. All you needed was a shiny car or a fast boat, and in Kermit's book you were a real hotshot.

I said, "Who knows if he's my daddy? Maybe he just sayin' so."

* * *

But he came back, and he wasn't just saying so. I didn't tell Grand or Grammie that I'd seen him; I pretended it hadn't happened. That was a mistake.

Two days later he came to our house. It was a Friday. Ever since the work started on Sapphire Island, Fridays had been noisy days in town, because that was payday for the men working on the development, and they had money to spend on drinking in the bars in town. At school I heard all kinds of stories about Friday night fights, and the police were busier than they ever used to be.

My father must have been in town and come out again, on his way to the trailers on the fenced storage area where some of the workers from Nassau were living. Or perhaps he was a security guard; I never found out. It was nearly bedtime when the car drove up. We'd been watching television, and I saw the headlights slant across the wall of the darkened room.

I went to the window and looked out. Grand came behind me. Three figures got out of the car, talking in loud voices that weren't quite loud enough to understand. A light flared as two of them lit cigarettes. In the moonlight, I saw them sit down on the little wall at the edge of our yard. The third man came toward the house, and in a moment there was a bang at the door.

"Don't go!" I said suddenly; I didn't know why.

Grand said reproachfully, "Could be somebody in trouble, Trey." And he went to the door.

I heard my father's voice, just like two days before, but slightly slurred now. "Hey, Father Peel, how you doin' today?"

There was a pause. Grand said slowly, "William. What I can do for you?"

"Came to see my child," my father said. Then he burped, loudly. "Pardon me," he said.

134

I was standing just inside the back room, in the shadows. Grammie came out past me, and squeezed my shoulder as she came. "You rest here," she whispered, and off she went to join Grand. I could see them standing there together like the two halves of a closed gate.

Grand said, "Technically you got two children in this house, William, but you been gone six years now, and not one word from you all that time. You switch off being a parent, you can't switch it on again like a tap."

"You done a good job, both of you," said my father in a lordly way. I could see him leaning against the door-jamb to prop himself up. "But you *grandparents*. Ain't no parents in this house. Lenore, she in Nassau—I back home now, earning good money. I seen my child Trey. Gettin' big now, needing a daddy. We talked." He burped again, more quietly. "Time I took over."

Lou had been in bed, but now I heard him padding across to join me. He stood there in his shorts listening, looking very small, big-eyed. I gave him a quick hug.

Grammie said briskly, "Go get youself a good night's sleep, William. You need one."

"I want Trey," my father said obstinately. "I got rights. Gonna take you to court."

I heard Lou's breathing begin to get faster. He gave a little whimper, and clutched at my arm.

Grand said quietly, "Just you try. You never married Lenore, you just give her two babies and walked out each time. Just you try goin' to court."

My father's voice began to rise. "I got friends!" he said loudly. "I got powerful friends, William Peel, and last time you tangled with them you got big trouble! You just watch out you don't find you got no boats at all!"

Lou was getting very agitated, right on the edge of a seizure; his arms and legs were trembling, and one shoulder beginning to jerk uncontrollably up and down.

"You can't stop me, old man!" my father yelled. "I goin' come take Trey, real soon!"

With that, Lou was over the edge. Gasping and grunting, he fell down on the ground in the worst seizure I'd ever seen, thrashing about, with spit running down his poor chin. I shrieked at my father, "Get out of here! Get out! Go away!" and I don't know if he heard me or not, because I was so busy then, and Grammie with me, tending to Lou and making sure he didn't bite his tongue, or break a leg, or bang his head on the floor.

By the time we had him calmed down and could get him back into bed, my father had gone, and his two friends with him.

When I kissed Grand good night, he took hold of my arm. "You didn't tell us you saw you daddy," he said gently.

"It was only for a minute or two," I said. "He stopped outside school and he said who he was, and he offered me a ride home and I said no. I didn't say anything to him like what he told you, and I sure don't need him. I hate him!"

Grand shook his head. He squeezed my arm, and let me go. "No you don't," he said. "You don't need him, but you don't hate him."

"He can't take me away, can he?" I hardly dared say it, I was so frightened it might be true.

"Never," Grand said. "Never, never, never."

One other thing was niggling at me, out of my father's drunken shouts. "You think he was one of the people who stole you boats?"

"Maybe," Grand said. "But he sure ain't gettin' my grandchild."

* * *

It was high summer now: hot, sticky weather, with no wind to stir the palms or the casuarinas. Quiet, ominous. The whole of my life then was ominous; I would wake up in the morning feeling frightened, waiting for something bad to happen. I had nightmares, though I could never remember the nightmares themselves, only the terrible fear that made me wake up trembling.

Everything seemed to be going wrong: Long Pond Cay was being destroyed, my father was threatening to take me away, and Lou wasn't well. He had recovered from that awful seizure without ill effects, after sleeping for twelve whole hours that night, but he was very quiet and sad. I often found him just sitting, staring into space.

I said to him one day, out on the porch, "Is it the Otherworld?"

He nodded.

"I'll do anything you want me to, Lou," I said, though I didn't look forward to it. "Do you know what to do?"

Lou shook his head, and looked sadder than ever. He reached into the pocket of his shorts and then held out his hand to me. The fossil star shell lay there on his palm.

I said, trying to understand, "It's time to take it to them?"

Lou nodded. But then he held up that same hand with two fingers upright. He stretched out the other hand, palm down, and made a fierce sideways movement with it, as if it were saying *no*. After that he held up the two fingers again.

I said slowly, "You can't go back, unless you have two stars to take."

Lou got to his feet and came and hugged me round the waist. The top of his head came up to my chin. Like I told you, he's not very big. I put my cheek on the top of his curly head for a moment and realized that the most important thing in the world, now, was not grieving over Long Pond Cay or worrying about my dangerous daddy. It was finding one more star shell that had been turned into rock by time.

* * *

So I did what I had done all my life when I had a real problem: I went to talk to Grand.

It was early the next morning, a Saturday. Grand had already left when I woke up, and I went down to the little marina to look for him. There he was, on the jetty, watching one of the bonefish boats take off for the day. Will was running the boat, as guide for two Americans who were peering eagerly ahead from under the peaks of their baseball caps. It was a beautiful day; the sky was clear blue and the water very still. A V-shape of ripples spread back toward us over the flat surface as the boat moved away. Will looked over his shoulder and waved to me before they disappeared into the mangroves.

Grand glanced down at me. His white beard looked a bit shaggier than usual; it needed trimming. "You up early," he said.

I said, "Wanted to ask you something."

He looked at me more closely. "You worried about you daddy?" he said. "Don't be. He got no chance at all of taking you away."

"Okay," I said.

Grand gave me a big reassuring smile. "Tell you what," he said. "I got an expedition to make today, out beyond the Plantation. You got much homework this weekend?"

"Done most of it already," I said. I'd written a story the night before for English, which is easy for me, not like algebra.

"Let's go," Grand said. "I doing pictures for the book. I'll take you and Lou. It's a long drive, mind. Think you'd like that?"

"Yes please!" I said. When Grand said "the book" he meant a history of Lucaya that a Bahamian friend of his at the University of Miami was writing. Grand was taking photographs for him, mostly of old settlements on the island that had been deserted for years. They weren't really old by the standards of Lou's star shell fossil, but this seemed a step in the right direction.

He said, "You wanted to ask me something?"

"Not now," I said. "You took care of it."

* * *

The Plantation is a settlement halfway down the island, past town, past my school, out where a lot of farming used to be done. Years and years ago, Grand says, after slavery was abolished and the cotton-growers were gone, people burned the scrub there and grew vegetables and fruit on the cleared land. But the soil is thin on our islands, and pretty soon they used up all its goodness and nothing would grow anymore. So they left their settlements and moved on, and their houses crumbled away and the vines and the scrub took the land back again. Here and there, you can find old foundations left, and that's what Grand wanted to photograph.

There's only one main highway on our island, one lane in each direction, and most of the way it runs along the northern shore. Once in a while you'll turn a bend and find yourself suddenly faced with a spectacular view of white beach and blue-green sea. The tourists love that, and you never get tired of it even if you live here and see it every day. Halfway to the Plantation we turned one of those corners, and Lou let out a surprised yelp.

But when I looked out, it wasn't just a pretty view he was seeing: it was a pair of ospreys, soaring over the water, traveling in the same direction as our car. Lou made his soft hooting sound, and almost as if it were an answer, we heard the ospreys piping their thin call to each other: *peeeu, peeeu* . . .

"Fish hawks up there," I said to Grand. "You think it's our pair from Long Pond Cay?"

"I doubt it," Grand said absently. He was busy keeping an eye out for the side road that led to the Plantation.

But Lou nodded, firmly. He kept looking up at the sky, even after the ospreys had drifted out of sight.

Although it was a really hot day, Grand had made us wear jeans and sneakers, with socks, because we were going to be in the bush, which is full of fierce prickly vines and shrubs as well as unfriendly kinds of spiders. He'd brought a machete with him, to carve a way through. A little while after he turned onto the Plantation road he found the place he wanted, where an overgrown trail led into the trees, and we followed him along it.

The bush thinned out after a bit, and we came across a piece of an old wall about three feet high, made of crumbling old blocks of limestone. A tree had grown out of it, and the roots had pushed some of the blocks to one side. Grand hacked away at the scrubby bushes until you could see the other three walls as well: a rectangle of tumbled blocks, the outline of a place that once, years and years ago, had been somebody's house. Grand had us stand there while he took pictures, so our height would be a measure.

Then we wandered off into the bush while he set up his tripod and took more pictures without us. I don't think either one of us was looking for a star shell here; we were just exploring. We weren't near the sea, and this had been a settlement of farmers, not fishermen. I took Grand's machete, which I'd been allowed to do for two years now, once he felt he could trust me not to cut off anybody's leg, including mine. I even had a smaller machete of my own, at home.

I was chopping a way through some branches throttled by the miserable wiry creeper that they call love vine, when I suddenly heard Lou shout. I put my head out of the branches, and saw him pointing upward.

There were the two ospreys again, swooping down over our heads, amazingly low. I'd never seen them so close before. They were wonderful: great grey-white wings spread wide, slowly flapping, banking sideways. One bird drifted above the other, then the other rose above the first, like a sort of dance. I couldn't imagine what they were doing here; they're birds of the sea and the shore, they live on fish. Were they hunting frogs or mice, for a change?

It was only when they began to whistle their fluting call every time they swooped over Lou that I realized they were trying to tell him something. Trying to lead him somewhere.

I came out into the open patch where he was standing and saw him moving forward, looking up, following the direction in which the great birds were slowly taking him. I went along beside him, doing my best to clear a way with the machete without damaging either of us.

"*Peeeu, peeeu,*" went one of the ospreys, and it swooped down and actually landed on the top of a seven-year apple tree about twenty yards ahead of us. Lou was making soft sounds to himself, excited, as he struggled through the bush. The bird stayed there, with its mate drifting to and fro overhead, as we got closer and closer. It took off only at the very last minute, when we came almost up to the tree.

Then we saw that the tree was growing out of the middle of another rectangle of broken-down walls, the ruin of another long-gone house, though higher than the one where we had left Grand.

The ospreys circled overhead, calling.

Lou went into the hollow of walls, and I followed him, pushing aside creepers with the machete.

I think we both saw it at the same time. In the center of the top block of crumbling lichen-patched limestone, in the tumbledown wall, there was a round gap like the one we had seen in the wall of the labyrinth, in the Otherworld, and in the gap was a small grey fossil star shell.

ELEVEN

Neither of us had the smallest doubt about what we had to do next, of course. When I had chipped the fossil shell out of the limestone with the tip of the machete, and Lou had put it carefully in his pocket with the other one, we went back toward Grand. He was already headed our way, so he spotted the second ruin, and was delighted.

"You can even see the doorway!" he said, and he spent about an hour taking photographs of it from every possible angle, while we fidgeted about, trying not to look impatient. Then on the way home he stopped in town and bought us both hamburgers as a reward, which was so unusual that he certainly wouldn't have believed us if we'd said we didn't want them. He saw several friends in the café, of course, and they all had a long gloomy chat about Long Pond Cay and told us how big we were growing. Those deep voices rumbled on and on till I thought we would never get home.

When we did, Lou slipped away to Grand's desk and

brought me the tide table. I knew we wouldn't get out of the house again that day; it gets dark before six at night in our islands. So I looked for next day's low tide, and it was in the middle of the afternoon.

"Two o'clock tomorrow," I said to Lou. "God spare life."

He grinned. That's what all the grown-ups say when they mean *cross fingers*.

I finished my weekend homework that night, to Grand and Grammie's surprise. We sat like quiet little angels in church next morning, and when we'd changed out of our good clothes I asked if Lou and I could go just one last time to Long Pond Cay.

"Please? Only for an hour or two. Pretty soon there'll be nothing left to see."

Grammie sighed. "That's true," she said. "For two pins I'd go with you, for a last look."

Lou was standing behind her, and he instantly looked so horrified I almost giggled. I said, "Uh—it's an awful small boat."

Grammie laughed her rolling deep laugh. "I wouldn't go in that little skiff of yours if I were a hundred pounds lighter," she said. "Off you go. But home before sunset, Trey."

Grand was busy at his desk, working out next month's bonefishing schedule. He glanced out of the window at the treetops. "Watch the wind," he said. "It may be shifting. And keep away from the development."

So we went to Long Pond Cay, and I didn't need telling to keep away from the end of the beach where development had begun; I was much too afraid my daddy might be there. When I think about it now, I wonder if danger was one of the things that brought our two worlds together, so close together that Lou and I could cross to and fro. Long Pond Cay was in danger of being changed forever; our family was in danger, from my father threatening to take me away. And Pangaia, if you could believe the Underground, was in danger of being completely wiped out. We were all linked together by threat.

It was a pretty day. I couldn't tell if the wind was really shifting, there was so little of it. A line of puffy little white clouds hung over the blue sky, and there was a low band of cloud on the horizon in the north, but nothing was moving. On the way out, I grabbed a hunk of bread from the kitchen and shoved it in the pocket of my shorts in case we needed a snack, and I took my machete.

I never did know quite why I took it. Maybe it was just in my mind from having used Grand's machete the day before.

Lou was so tense with excitement, it was as if electricity was coming out of him. He sat up in the bow, staring ahead at the water. I headed out a long way offshore, toward the far end of the long white bay, though our dinghy draws so little water there was no chance of us going aground even at this low tide. It wasn't the shallows that I was trying to avoid, it was anyone from

Sapphire Island Resort. Since it was Sunday, I hoped there'd be nobody around.

We were out in open water when I saw the power-boat. It was roaring down the newly dredged channel between Lucaya and Long Pond Cay, going so fast that its wake, curving up from the stern, was the thing I saw first. It seemed to be heading for the open sea, but then it slowed down, and the wake dropped. They'd seen us. After a moment the boat curved round and began heading in our direction.

I pushed the engine up to full throttle but it was hopeless: a little fifteen-horse outboard is like a newborn puppy compared to a big powerboat. And this one had the long bow and pointy shape of a cigarette boat, the high-speed boats that are called by that name because they're so skinny and fast. There used to be a lot of ciga-rette boats in the islands when I was very tiny, in the big days of drug smuggling. Planes would fly over from South America at night and drop floating packages of drugs in the water, in amongst the dozens of little cays on the south side of Lucaya, and the boats would come out at first light and pick them up. A really powerful cigarette boat could get to Florida with a million-dollar load of drugs in half a day. Grand said he'd come across one when he was bonefishing, once: a huge sleek grey ciga-rette boat hidden in the mangroves, waiting for its owner to jump into it at dawn.

The boat came roaring up to us, and Lou scrambled

back toward me from the bow, staring. There were three men in the little cockpit, behind that enormous bow full of engine. They were all Bahamian, and one of them was our father.

He was standing behind the man at the wheel, with a beer can in his hand. He was laughing. "Little Trey!" he bellowed. "I got you! You comin' with me!"

"Come to Daddy, baby!" yelled one of the other men, and I knew they were all drinking, and maybe all of them drunk.

Lou was hunched right back by me in the stern of the dinghy, and I was still going full speed toward Long Pond Cay, though the powerboat was keeping level with me without even trying. The man driving the boat nudged up its speed a little and began curving round ahead, to cut me off.

You have to understand one of the things about my daddy. Some of it I only know from Mam telling me. He took off and left her after I was born, and then when I was about five years old he came back again, and said he loved her and he would stay. Around then is the time of that photograph I saw, I guess. She looked happier than she does now. But then Lou was born, and he went off again. The worst thing was that because Lou looks more like Mam than I do, with the darker skin, he refused to believe he was Lou's daddy. Specially when it turned out Lou didn't talk. He paid him no attention, just as if he didn't exist—even though he is Lou's daddy, certain sure.

And it was the same thing today. He was pretending Lou wasn't even in that boat—and if he could have got hold of me he would have left him there alone, seven years old, alone on the sea.

"Trey!" he yelled. "Come on here, baby baby!"

There was just one thing I could do.

"Hold on, Lou!" I said, and I turned hard to one side so that we shot past the stern of the big boat as it was curving to cut us off from the shore. We bumped over its wake, and then I was heading for the shore across a part of the bay where the water was so shallow nobody would ever cross it at low tide. I knew the powerboat couldn't get over it without hitting the sand, and I wasn't even positive that we could, but it was worth trying.

We whizzed along, over water so shallow you could see the white sand clear through it. I looked over my shoulder and saw that the big boat had turned to come after us, but that sure enough it was stuck. What I didn't see, at that moment, was that my daddy had jumped overboard and was swimming after us.

Even our little propellor hit sand before long, so I cut the motor and we both jumped into the water and pulled the two anchors out to the full length of their lines, at each end of the boat. Then we set them in the sand so the boat would float up and stay there when the tide rose. Lou knew just what to do without being told, and we were very quick—but not quite quick enough.

I grabbed my machete out of the boat, and we ran. We

splashed through the shallows and ran up the beach, and into the tall oat grass on the dunes. I looked back to check the boat, and saw my father stumbling ashore on to the sand. He could see us; he was yelling. He began to run after us.

We plowed up through the dry sand, as fast as we could. A dozen things were darting around my mind. Where could we go? He could catch us by sea, he could catch us by land—Long Pond Cay was Sapphire Island Resort now, where he worked with his powerful friends. The way we were running, we were headed only for the flats, where the soft mud would catch our feet. We'd have to go sideways instead, along the edge of the flats, away from the new development and over to the windy seaward end of the cay, where a ridge of trees grew.

I called to Lou, "Go left! This way!" and as I turned past the casuarinas fringing the dunes, I tripped and went sprawling on the sand. The machete flew out of my hands and into a bush. Lou saw me fall, and came back to help. I shrieked at him to run, but he kept coming. I scrambled up, and groped around in the bush for my machete.

Overhead I heard that familiar thin cry, "*Peeeu, peeeu,*" and knew that the ospreys were wheeling about, high up, watching.

My fingers found the handle of the machete, and I was up on my feet again, turning inland. My father came running over the dunes, among the casuarina trees. Ahead of me, Lou let out a strange high hooting sound that I'd never heard before; it echoed eerily over the gleaming mirror-still bonefish flats.

I could hear my father's heavy breathing as he ran at me. Suddenly I was paralyzed; I turned desperately forward and back and didn't know which way to go. I faced my father, holding out my machete like a sword, and stood there screaming at him. "Get away! Get away!"

He paused for a moment, panting, his face stiff with anger.

And a wind sang in the casuarina trees, and the air shivered all around us. I felt Lou take my free hand. The light was dying, and I knew that the Otherworld was there behind me, and that one more step would put me there, out of reach. So I reached my foot backwards.

My daddy's face changed. His eyes widened, and his mouth opened a little way in horror, or astonishment, or plain disbelief. I don't think he saw the Otherworld, I don't think you can see it touching ours unless it's calling you. I think we simply vanished away from him.

And he vanished from us, and Lou and I were standing in half-darkness, in cold air, at the entrance to the labyrinth.

* * *

In the beginning nobody was there, not Bryn nor Gwen nor Annie. Two lighted lanterns were on the ground, filling the tunnel with dim light. Our shadows were huge on the roof. We stood there facing the rough, damp stone wall, with the three engraved words above our heads, and beside them the three round holes with a small rock star in the first.

> *Rigel*
> *Bellatrix*
> *Betelgeuse*

We were still gasping for breath after the running and the fear, yet some other things from our own time were quite gone. Though our clothes had been soaked from splashing through the sea, and our sneakers heavy with seawater and sand, now they were dry. The hunk of bread in my pocket was dry too, though it should have been squishy and soaked. So was the machete in my hand. I noticed these things without wondering about them; the front of my mind was too busy feeling relief that now my daddy couldn't carry me away from Lou. But right on the heels of that came the other fear, the one that belonged to the Otherworld: what was the thing that we had to do here?

That seemed never to have frightened Lou, and it didn't now. He reached into the pocket of his shorts, and brought out the two fossil star shells: little chunks of grey rock in the shape of ten-pointed stars. Holding them out to me, he looked up at the two round gaps in the wall, and made a little questioning sound.

"I know," I said. "They need to go in those holes, for sure, but how do we get them there? No way we can reach, even with me holding you up."

Lou was still staring up at the gaps, thinking. He turned to me, facing me, and patted me on the shoulders. Then he bent and patted his feet.

"Hmm," I said. I didn't think that would work. But when I went and stood next to the wall and reached up both my arms, my fingers weren't much more than a foot from the nearest hole. And Lou was a lot taller than the length of my arms. He was right; if we could get him up to stand on my shoulders, he could reach.

This was something we'd never done before. I crouched down facing the wall, with my hands flat against it, and Lou tried to get a foot on my shoulder. He couldn't, it was too far up. Then he tried to do it by standing on my knee first, and I fell down, and so did he. He laughed. I'd banged my knee, so I didn't laugh right that minute, but I wasn't going to give up yet.

"Try sitting on my shoulders," I said. We knew how to do that—at any rate, we'd done it a lot in the sea, fooling around. I got down again, and Lou cocked his leg over the back of my neck and grabbed my head, so that he was more or less sitting on my shoulders, and with a lot of effort, and him clutching at the wall as well as my head, I managed to stagger up to standing. He was a whole lot heavier than he'd felt when we did it in the water, I can tell you. But he made a little crowing sound, and I could tilt my head just enough to see him fit one of the star shells into the lowest gap in the wall.

There was a tiny, spooky flash of light, and a click,

and the shell was resting in the gap. But though he stretched as high as he could, he couldn't reach up to the third hole to put the last shell in place.

That was the moment when we heard a rustling, thudding sound behind us: the sound of feet running. I felt a crazy flash of fear that my father had somehow been transported to the Otherworld, to chase and catch me, but as the feet skidded close we heard Bryn's voice, deep and urgent.

"Wait, Lou! Wait a moment!"

He was level with us now, and he swung Lou up off my shoulders. But instead of reaching him up higher, he set him down on the ground. Annie was there too, and Gwen, in the same rough dark clothes as before. They all three looked worried, and very serious; I suppose they'd been afraid they might not reach us in time. In time for what?

Annie crouched beside Lou so that she was looking him in the eye. She took him by the shoulders. She said, "Are you quite sure?"

Lou laughed, as if she had made a joke. He nodded, very hard.

Gwen said softly into my ear, "You see, this is a danger that you are going into. This mystery of the words on the wall."

I heard myself say, "For love of life."

She still looked serious, but she punched me lightly on the arm, like saying *right on.* We really could have been friends, Gwen and me, in spite of her being older. She said, "And you came out of danger this time, didn't you, you came running. I felt it."

She was looking at the machete in my right hand, but without asking. "It's a long story," I said.

Gwen turned her head to look at Lou. "Stay beside him," she said. "Stay beside him all the time."

Annie was hugging Lou now, very close, the way Mam hugs us when she has to go back to Nassau. When she was done, Bryn put a hand on his shoulder too and gave it a squeeze. His face was grave and stern, and—it's an odd word, considering Lou's only seven—*respectful*. I was beginning to feel more and more as though the Underground didn't think of us as people, but as some kind of offering to Gaia. Whoever Gaia was.

They are fanatics, do you understand that? Sir had said. *Fanatics . . . threatening doom . . . threatening a sacrifice . . .*

But Lou trusted them, so I had to as well.

Bryn lifted Lou up high; he was so big that Lou could sit there on just one of his broad shoulders, with his hand round Bryn's head. Gwen gave me a quick peck on the cheek. "Go well," she said.

Annie came to stand beside me with one hand on my shoulder. And Lou reached out from his high perch and fitted the third star shell into its gap on the wall. Like the other, it flashed and clicked, and there it was, in place, as if it had always been there.

But that wasn't all.

Very gradually, a deep rumbling sound began, some-where a long way below us. It wasn't too loud, but it was *huge*; you could feel a faint vibration in the earth and the rock all around. It gave me a hollow feeling in the pit of my stomach, the feeling you have when you're empty, except that the emptiness this time was full of fear.

Bryn put up his hands to Lou and swung him down to the ground. Lou looked round for me, and reached out to take my free hand, and I saw Bryn, Annie and Gwen all stepping back away from us.

There we stood, the two of us, alone.

The rumbling died down, and in the wall, the three star shells began to glow. Brighter and brighter they grew, blazing out, filling the cave with brilliant light, and then with a tremendous cracking noise, a split opened in the wall beside them. Very slowly, with the awful scraping screech we had heard when Bryn opened the first rock door, the wall started to move, but this time it swung back like a door on a hinge. The stars were in the middle of this door, and as it swung, the light blazing out of them filled the dark space of the labyrinth.

He walks through stars, the prophecy had said.

I felt Lou's hand give mine a little squeeze, and we walked in.

Our shadows went before us into the cave. It was wider than the tunnels had been, though not so high, maybe six feet or so. The rocky walls were bumpy but smooth, gleaming with moisture. It smelled damp, but the air was fresh; there must have been little gaps open to the air, somewhere.

I heard a noise ahead, and I stopped. I could feel my heart thumping. "Listen!"

Lou cocked his head, but there was nothing but a faint dripping of water. He tugged my hand.

"Lou," I said, not moving, "didn't they tell you what this is all *for*? Are we going in here to find something?"

Lou looked up at me earnestly, and shook his head.

The handle of my machete was damp with my own sweat. "We just go in? And what happens, happens?"

He nodded. Then he flashed a grin at me, and he pointed his finger ahead, and then back, behind us. *We go in, we come out.*

Let's hope so, Lou.

He tugged my hand again. That talking tree had certainly given him total faith in what we were doing. Total blind faith. I swallowed, and we went on. The cave turned sharply to the left, so we followed it, and the light came with us. I don't know how. It didn't behave like normal beams of light; it seemed to be filling the space all around us, like air.

Our footsteps made soft scuffling noises. We turned another corner, this time to the right. I'd expected the labyrinth to be a maze, where you had to choose the right way to get to the center, and then follow it back again to get out, but this wasn't a maze, it was just a twisty cave. And now that the dim light was all around us, not coming from any one place, we had no shadows.

Just as we came to another dark turning, there was a high squeal from somewhere ahead, and I saw a pair of red eyes shining in the darkness, down on the ground. I let out a yell, and we stopped. The light flowed round us. There against the wall was a black rat, as big as my foot. The red eyes gleamed at us. I could see sharp bright teeth.

Lou let go of my hand and reached awkwardly into the pocket of my shorts. He pulled out the chunk of bread that was still in there, squished but dry, and he threw it onto the ground behind us. The rat rushed past us to get it, brushing by my ankle, and as it got there we heard more squeals, and two other rats dived at the bread out of the darkness. The squeals became angry snarls, and yelps of pain, and we left them tearing not just at the bread but at each other.

The luminous air came with us round the bend. It was a strange half-light, just enough to show the direction of the cave, not enough to show details—which made it scary, because you could imagine monsters in every patch of shadow. I could, anyway. Lou, he just went on.

And then, round the next turning, we came on something with a light of its own. It was the light that we saw first, glowing out of the left-hand wall ahead of us: a wonderful luminous glow of rainbow colors all flowing in and out of each other, the way colors do on the surface of a soap bubble. It was so beautiful that I forgot to be scared; I was too busy wondering what such a light could possibly be coming from. When we came closer we saw that there was a tall niche, almost a small room, in the wall, from which this light was pouring, and that the thing inside it was even more amazing than the light itself.

It was as if the softest imaginable blanket, very light and thick, woven of long silky iridescent fibres, had been attached to the back of the niche and then molded around the sides. If it hadn't been upright, it would have looked like a wonderful welcoming nest, inviting you to curl up in its coziness. Even the way it was, you wanted to walk into it and nestle up against the sides. The threads shifted very gently, glimmering. I put out a hand, but couldn't quite bring myself to touch, in case the thing, whatever it was, might vanish like a bubble and suddenly be gone.

But Lou reached out and grabbed my hand, hard, and pulled it down. He gave a hard sharp grunt of warning.

And before there was time for anything else, the center of this beautiful feathery nest fell away, as if it had dissolved, and out of the opening came a nightmare. Stalking toward us we saw a sprawl of hairy black legs as tall as Lou, and from them hung a gleaming black head and a huge round body, glittering black with a bright red mark on its belly. It was a gigantic spider, half as big as me. She was horrible. Her long legs swung her body over to us so fast that there wasn't the smallest chance of escape.

One black leg kicked me hard in the chest, and I fell backwards, dropping my machete, banging my head on the rock. Through my dizziness I heard Lou scream, and as I scrambled to my feet I saw the spider towering over him, two bristled black legs flickering to and fro, an iridescence like the light glittering through the air. He struggled only for a second. She was wrapping him in spider-silk. Her spinning-legs moved so fast that already I could only see his head.

I had no time, and I knew it. I picked up the machete and slashed at her. The first hit cut off one of her spinning-legs. It dropped away like a broken branch. The spider stopped weaving and for a stunned moment she didn't move. That was the luckiest moment of my entire life. I held the machete high in both my hands and brought it down as hard as I could, and the one stroke split her head and then cut her belly open almost in two. The machete smashed against the rock as it came down, and the impact made me stagger.

The spider made no sound. An awful-smelling green goo spurted out of her belly as the body fell backwards, and the legs flailed and twitched. I tried desperately to keep out of their way, because as I looked at her now, something jumped out of my memory. In our islands, the most dangerous spider is one called the bottle spider, or sometimes the black widow, and the way you can tell her is that she is black with a red marking on her belly the shape of an hourglass. If one of her stinging-legs gets you, you can die.

And that's when she's only the size of my little fingernail.

That huge disgusting body jerked violently once more, and inside it, along with all the green stuff, I glimpsed a cluster of small white things, all pressed together. I think they must have been eggs, like when you cut open a fish you've caught and find the roe, the mass of eggs the fish would have laid if you hadn't caught it. I feel sorry when I've killed hundreds of unborn fish, but I sure didn't feel sorry about the unborn spiders. A wave of the smell from the spider's guts hit me, and I retched, and threw up on the rocky floor.

Lou was lying beside me, all trussed up in spider-silk. I was terrified she might have stung him; he wasn't moving, and his eyes were closed. I thought desperately: *don't spiders wrap up insects to keep them alive?*

"Lou!" I said. "Lou! Look at me!"

I gazed at his face, praying. After a moment his eyelids flickered, and he was blinking at me.

"Oh thank God," I said, and I picked up my machete, wiped it on my shorts, and went to rip the spider-silk off Lou's body. I thought it would be easy; I just slipped the end of the machete blade under the first few strands and gave a little flick.

They wouldn't budge. They were so fine you could hardly see them, those tiny strands, but they might have been made of steel wire. My machete is pretty sharp, but I couldn't cut even one strand, however hard I sawed at it. Lou was wrapped so close, his arms against his body, his legs tight together, that there was no way I could use the machete like an ax to chop through the silk, not without chopping at him too.

I knew that wouldn't have worked anyway. When you touched the stuff, it was soft and gentle and stroky, just the way that glimmering nest in the wall looked. But it was stronger than steel, or stone, or fiberglass, or fish line, or anything I'd ever seen on earth. Nothing could cut it, nothing at all.

A great wave of hopelessness suddenly swallowed me up, and I heard myself let out a noise I didn't know I could make, a long shriek of rage and fear and despair. More than anything else I think I was screaming for help—in a place where nobody could hear me, nobody cared, nobody would come. Then I choked up, and started to cry.

So I didn't hear the first small rustling sounds, because my own sobbing was in my ears. The light was very dim in the cave now. The moment the spider had died, that beautiful iridescence in its gleaming wall-nest had died too, so that the only light around us was that faint glow in the air that had come with us from the beginning. In both directions, everything else was shadow.

And out of the shadows at the far end, beyond the spider's nest, came a host of little flickering dark shapes as soft as moths, as quiet as falling leaves, dancing through the air. They flew jerkily, silently, darting round our heads. In a ghostly throng they hovered around Lou and tugged gently at the ends of the spider-silk that bound him, pulling it away from him, nudging him to his feet so that they could spin him round and round as they pulled the fine terrible strands away.

They were little brown bats, a great crowd of bats, light and fragile, and as they worked I thought once or twice that I could hear a high whispering twittering amongst them. But then it would be gone, and I felt I had imagined it. They filled the air with their tiny bodies and their delicate membrane-wings; there was a fluttering brown cloud all around me, and yet not one small body even brushed my face.

I stood very still, hardly breathing, my cheeks still wet. And there stood Lou before me, free of the spider-silk, eyes wide and bright, smiling.

We hugged each other, and for an instant I heard the high twittering voices in my ear like joy. Then there was only the rustling, the sense of a flickering brown cloud persistent all around us, filling the air. They weren't going away, they were in charge of us, they wanted us to pay attention. But to what?

Lou stood there with his head up, and his eyes closed. It was as if he was listening to them, though there was nothing but the soft rustling to be heard. He began to walk, slowly. I knew it must be the way the host of bats were taking us and I walked with him. The light that had always been with us faded out of the air and was gone. We were in the dark now, in the kingdom of the bats, moving where they wanted us to move.

From the ground, I heard a brief scurrying, of quick feet rushing by. The rats must have got scent of the spider. In a moment they were gone.

Then Bryn's voice came out of the darkness. "Lou? Trey?"

"Bryn," I said. I was walking in a slow daze, walking where the fluttering guardians round my head took me, and it didn't even seem surprising that Bryn was there. I assumed the bats had somehow fetched him too.

"Is Lou," Bryn said, his voice husky, "is Lou—" and he couldn't finish the sentence but I knew what he wanted to say, and I thought I knew why.

"Lou's alive," I said coldly. "Lou's here."

That is, I hoped that he was there, because we were separate now, no longer holding hands. We were alone in the dark, together.

And then the bats whirled in a frenzy in front of us, making us stop. We had come to the place where we were meant to be, and it was all so strange that it's hard to find normal words to tell what it was like.

There was no light, and yet I felt I could see. Perhaps I was seeing only what was put into my mind. I thought I saw a kind of rounded space in the darkness, gleaming a little the way the inside of a big soup-pot or cauldron might gleam, and in the center of the round gleaming space I saw a woman's head. Only her face, and that very hazily. It was the way I've seen a face in a dream, and known that it was a particular familiar person, Grammie or Mr. Ferguson or Kermit, even though it was a face I'd never seen before.

This was a face I had never seen, a woman with kind eyes and a strong mouth, and I knew it was someone I had never known and yet had always known. I can't tell you what that means now that I am back here, but I understood then, there. The face was Gaia.

She spoke to us. It was like the voice of the whole earth.

"You mistake me always. You dream of monsters, who will kill your heroes. No! No monsters are needed. I asked not for sacrifice, but for renewal."

I think she was talking to Bryn, and he answered her. His voice was shaking, full of astonishment.

"But it was in the prophecy," he said. "*Out of the labyrinth the weaver spins him.* She was a Wilderness creature, and our people have had her below, for generations. They told us that was what the prophecy meant. I was born Spiderkeeper, taught to keep her alive. Throw in food through the airholes, keep her there, to weave Lugh through death to life."

So he had sent us into the labyrinth knowing the spider would kill us, expecting Lou to be magically reborn, to somehow save their world. They had all done that, all the Underground people, even Gwen. Had we never been anything to them but a sacrifice?

Gaia sighed, in a great deep rumble that came through the earth like thunder. "Mankind," she said with distaste. "The last species. So ingenious, so foolish. Hear now, man, and understand. Lugh followed his instructions. He passed through the stars into the dark labyrinth, so that I might bear him up to the light, as I bear every sprouting seed. But the weaver of his rebirth is not a great monstrous spider, it is a child."

Bryn said, bemused, "A *child?*"

"Children weave story," said Gaia's rumbling voice. "Wait, and watch. From child to child the right words go, and are preserved, even as the child dies by becoming man or woman."

"Forgive me," Bryn said. "Forgive us."

"I forgive, but at a price," Gaia said. "At a price. Many will die, but all will be renewed. Go up, and you will see."

The eyes in the shadowy face glinted blue, green, brown, all colors, and they were fixed on Lou. And it was not Louis Peel from Lucaya that they were seeing.

"Go up, brave Lugh," she said. "Go up to my Lughnasa games. It is the day to dance with the children, in the story as old as time."

The long low growling under the earth grew suddenly into a crashing roar, and above our heads the rock split open. Up and up the split ran, bursting, cracking, until you could see a chink of daylight at the top.

In the darkness below, there was a busy rustling on all sides, from all directions. The host of little brown bats filled the air again, flickering about us, and each one of them brought a strand of spider-silk—from the wrapping that had held Lou, from the soft nest in the wall, maybe even from the dead spider herself. They released the fine strands into the air, and in the glimmer of light from above we saw all these iridescent threads merge into a shining knotted rope, rising up, rising.

As if an invisible hand pulled it, the slender, shining rope rose up to the daylight, and hung there, still, without swaying. Lou went to it and began to climb, holding the rope with hands and feet, and I put down my machete on the rocky ground and climbed after him.

TWELVE

We climbed and climbed up the rope, pulling with hands, pushing with feet, from knot to knot. My arms and shoulders were screaming at me by the time we reached the top. Above me I saw Lou tumble sideways off the rope, into daylight. I hoisted myself the last few feet and tumbled after him, and found myself rolling on sandy dirt. Bryn's head rose up out of the split in the ground behind us.

We were on a rocky hillside, overlooking a town. You could see that most of it was new, still being built. The part right below us looked old, with roofs and terraces spread in rows down to a kind of square, and a road running down from that to a harbor, and a glimpse of grey sea. I could only see a little piece of the harbor, because most of it was hidden by the hill on which we stood.

Inland, though, you could see slope after slope of new houses, covering every foot of land, and in the distance, chunky machines standing on the next sandy brown hill, waiting to chop down its few scrubby trees and replace them with buildings and roads. The horizon beyond disappeared into a rim of brown fog, under the hazy Pangaian sky where the sun always looked furry, even on a fine day.

I heard music from below, jolly music, with bright trumpets and jingly tunes, and I realized that the square down there was filled with people. Lou was already scrambling over the rocks toward a path that led downward, and I went after him. I no longer cared much whether Bryn was following, but I knew he was; I could hear his sliding feet.

The first streets we came to were empty, but as we went farther down we began to catch up with people walking: a couple here or there, then a family, then more, all hurrying down toward the square. Bryn was walking with us now, and a chunky, youngish woman with two little girls skipping beside her glanced at him and smiled. I suppose he was a striking sight, with his tall broad-shouldered figure and his golden beard. She had a friendly face and she included us in the smile; she was one of those people who just like to talk.

"With any luck, the speeches will be over," she said.

Bryn said amiably, "I hope so."

She laughed. "They do so like to make themselves sound grand, don't they? *Incorporation of Greater Harbiton*—as if it was anything more than making the town bigger and bigger."

"And bigger and bigger," said Bryn.

One of the small girls was skipping with a rope, murmuring some rhyme to herself as she skipped, keeping pace with us. The other, smaller, was hopping along on one foot, kicking a round stone. She nudged it over to Lou, and Lou kicked it gently back, and they hopped happily along together, grinning, kicking.

"It's nice to have the space, though," the woman said. "The girls with their own room. Did you move out of the city too?"

"Oh yes," said Bryn. "Indeed we did."

"Nice to have the space," she said again, contentedly. "And this was all desert, after all." She looked fondly at the little girl and Lou, hopping along kicking their stone. "Are yours looking forward to the games?"

She was asking Bryn, but she was smiling at me, so I smiled back. "Sure," I said.

We turned a corner, and suddenly we were part of a crowd of cheerful people in the square, which looked much bigger now that we were in it. Big grey stone buildings ran along its edge, with alleyways leading off into a mixture of brick-walled houses and glass-walled office blocks. At one end of the square, people were applauding, as a bunch of official-looking men and women climbed down from a platform. A band was playing. I glanced nervously at two or three groups of security police, in the dark red uniforms, but they all seemed very relaxed and cheerful and paid us no attention.

The music stopped, and people began drifting to the

edge of the square, leaving a growing space in the center.

"Just in time!" the woman with us said happily, and her two little girls ran out into the space. The smaller one looked back at Lou. She was a cute little girl, with two bows in her hair.

"Come on!" she called.

Lou waved to her, but stayed beside me, near Bryn and their mother.

And out into the center of the square, dozens of children came running. Maybe hundreds. I don't know where they came from; they just appeared from all over, slipping out of the crowd, out from alleyways and round corners. They were very young; they looked to be about Lou's age, boys and girls together, and suddenly they were playing a game. It was an odd game, a kind of chain-tag. I hadn't played anything like it for years; I'd almost forgotten how it went.

I think now that this is what Gaia meant when she said children were the weavers of story. We all have these rhymes and games that we learn from other kids when we're small, and the younger ones learn them from us, and so on. But when we grow up, we forget them. Only the little ones keep carrying them on, only the little ones know them.

It started with one skinny girl in a black jumpsuit, waving her arms and screeching out to them all. She was holding a raggedy blue cap in one hand, like a baseball cap. When enough of them were watching her, waiting, she yelled, "Blue Man, rise up!" and she dropped the blue cap on the head of a little chubby boy nearby.

The kids all scattered then, and the little boy in the cap chased them. Round and round the space they went, with the adults cheering. When the boy caught someone, he kept hold of his hand and they chased the rest together, until there were three chasing, and then four, and in the end a whole chain. Only the ones at either end could tag someone, so there was a lot of ducking and dodging and laughter.

As they ran, they sang an odd little song, and skipped in time to it so that their running was almost like a dance.

> *"Run catch the year*
> *Run catch the sun*
> *Year turn round for everyone,*
> *Up in the sky*
> *Down in the ground*
> *Catch him up till the year turn round!"*

The twisting line of children wove its way in and out of the edge of the crowd, around the square, right past us, and the boy in the blue cap reached out and tagged Lou, so that he had to join the line at the very end. It made me nervous, but Lou flashed me a grin and skipped off after the rest.

To and fro they went, until there wasn't a little one

left who wasn't in the long, singing, skipping chain. Then the tall skinny girl popped out of nowhere again holding a bright yellow cap, and put it on the head of the last one in line, a small girl with long fair braids.

"Yellow Man, rise up!" she shouted, even though the chosen one was a girl, and at once all the children dropped hands and scattered, and the little girl chased after them and the chain began to grow again. They danced round and round, in and out. I saw Lou dodging, laughing, till he was the very last child tagged to join the long snaking line.

And the skinny girl was there again, this time with a green cap. She held it high for a moment. Then she dropped it on Lou's head and shouted, "Green Man, rise up!"

For an instant I remembered Gaia's voice: *From child to child the right words go . . .*

And what happened then was so impossible to believe that I have trouble writing it down.

The children stood still, wherever they happened to be, and all together they shouted,

> *"Up in the sky*
> *Down in the ground*
> *Catch him up till the year turn round!*
> *Green Man, rise up!"*

The shout faded away into nothing and there was

dead silence, with everyone in that great grey square still as statues, and into the silence a wind came, first murmuring like the breath of casuarinas and then growing, whining. It lifted the edges of people's clothes, it blew litter round the streets, and as it blew, everybody near my little brother Lou backed away from him until he was alone, in a space. I couldn't see his face, it was shadowed by the brim of the green hat, but I saw him begin to change.

He began to grow.

He grew, and he grew, the little cap falling away as his head grew, until he was a creature ten feet tall, fifteen feet tall, twenty feet tall, all green. He was the Green Man they had called up, with a huge green face that was not Lou's face but a grown man's, with its mouth wide, laughing. Green leaves and curling tendrils were growing out of his head; he had branches for hair, twigs for eyebrows; branches were growing out of all his body as if he were a great bush, and when he held out his hands, leaves grew from his massive fingers, long shoots, twirling as they grew.

I watched. I can't tell you what I felt. It was like being frozen, paralyzed. Behind me, I heard Bryn give a little sigh.

The Green Man opened his mouth wider yet, as his enormous body stretched further and further up, high as the buildings all around, and out of this mouth poured a great torrent of branches and vines and leaves, like a green waterfall. It flowed over the pavement and the streets, and as it came I heard a rumbling and a crackling begin, as everywhere in the big open square, and in the streets around it, sharp green sprouts came breaking up out of stone and concrete and brick, bursting up, cracking the paved ways. Inside the buildings of the town there was a deeper rumbling, and people came running out of doorways as branches sprouted from windows, and cracked walls, and sent tiles tumbling down from roofs.

I saw nobody hurt; it was as if the green flood were trying to avoid people, though I don't know if that was possible in the end. In a moment or two the stunned city began to defend itself, and several of those little black helicopters came swooping low out of the hazy sky, over the square. Two of them hovered near the great Green Man, and dropped some sort of explosives, bombs I suppose. They burst near enough to make the enormous figure lurch, but in the same instant, huge snaking green vines shot up from the ground and snatched the helicopters out of the sky. They crashed into the square and burst into flames, and I saw the other helicopters drop and explode too.

I heard a different rumbling then, over the noise of the green things breaking the city apart, and down the streets that led into the square came armored grey vehicles like big lumbering steel boxes, huge and menacing. There were slits in their sides, and out of the slits came jets of blazing white light, that leaped out at the springing branches and fried them, where they touched, into blackened stumps. But they were no match for the flood of leaves and vines and branches pouring out of the earth all around them. In spite of the rays of fire, that advancing green mass wrapped itself round every single vehicle, rocking it, turning it over, putting out its light and fire. There was no stopping the force of the Green Man.

He towered into the sky, a huge square figure like a dense wood of interweaving green trees, and out of his great open laughing mouth now came flowers, a flood of flowers, roses, anemones, hibiscus, hundreds of others, and all of them red. In a scarlet river they poured down the streets, and were caught up by little streams, where water ran fast through the gutters of the street from broken water mains. Red they ran, these flower-filled streams, through the square and down the main street to the harbor steps. Looking down the slope to the harbor I could see them spreading out over the sea in streaks of red.

The sky was growing darker out there over the sea, and waves were springing up, rocking the lines of bobbing red blossoms. Lightning flickered from the horizon. I heard a low growl of thunder, far off. Something made me turn inland, to look at the horizon there, and everywhere on the rolling hills, with their endless grey buildings, there was a new haze of green. Over all the land; over all Pangaia, perhaps.

Bryn was at my side suddenly, exultant, eyes blazing, as the Green Man towered above us and the flood of green branches and red flowers poured down and around. The air was full of shouts and screams, and the crackling and rumbling of stone burst apart by the growing green things. Bryn yelled in my ear, clutching my shoulder hard.

"Any moment from now, any moment, the worlds will touch!" he shouted. "Watch and go, Trey! Watch for Lou!"

But how could I watch for my little brother Lou? Lou was the Green Man!

"Watch!" Bryn yelled. "Save him, one last time, as he has saved Pangaia!" His fingers dug into my shoulder so hard that it hurt. I felt his beard against my neck as he yelled in my ear, "Thank you, Trey! Gaia go with you!"

I looked up, to try to see any trace of Lou left in that huge figure, but in the same moment I was knocked off my feet by another wave of branches and leaves and flowers, pouring down, filling the street. I couldn't see Bryn, I couldn't see anything but a blur of green, as I was carried along, struggling, away from the square and toward the harbor. Twigs scratched my legs, vines wrapped themselves lovingly round my hands; it was like being caught in dense scrubland at home on the island, except that everything was moving. The leaves parted for a moment above my head, and I thought I caught a glimpse of the Green Man, but there was no longer a recognizable figure up there, only a dense mass of trees like a towering wood.

Then the leafy green tide dropped me, and I found

myself on hands and knees on the stony shore, with the
sound of a rising wind in my ears. Leaves and branches
whipped past me, with wet seaweed twined in them, and
there was a strong smell of the sea. I could see the sky,
the hazy grey-brown sky of Pangaia, with clouds riding
across it—

* * *

—and then that shimmering came again, the shaking
of the air that was always the sign of our crossing
between the other world and our own. For a moment I
could see nothing but a blur, and the sound in my ears
changed, grew louder, became the sound of wind in
casuarina branches higher than I'd ever heard it, like the
shriek of an animal.

And I was on the beach of Long Pond Cay, with sand
under my fingers instead of stones, and small choppy
waves were splashing at me as the tide began to rise. Out
on the water just offshore, our little dinghy was tossing at
anchor.

In the moment I saw the boat I reacted out of
instinct, knowing I had to let out the line to match the
rising tide. I splashed out toward it, and saw that the sea
all round me was scattered with leaves and broken
twigs, and red blossoms, hibiscus and poinciana and
bougainvillea, even though there was nowhere on that
wild little island they could have come from. Sunshine
flickered between mounds of grey-white cloud running
across the sky. I reached the boat, with water up to my

neck, and tugged the anchor-line loose so that the boat swung free. Then I hauled it in toward shallower water so that I could climb in.

I looked up. Out past the boat, among the waves tossing the twigs and the scattered blossoms, I saw Lou.

He was swimming toward me; all I could see was his curly black head. It was as if my whole mind suddenly came to life again. I gave a yell and let go of the boat, and half-splashed, half-swam toward him, until we were both in water shallow enough to stand, clutching each other. "Lou—oh Lou—"

He was coughing and spluttering as if he were half-drowned, and he was exhausted. I had to hold him up in the water. There was no way of telling whether he had any memory whatsoever of the Green Man. He was my little brother again, a frightened small boy now. And he was as naked as on the day he was born.

THIRTEEN

I got us into the boat, somehow, and that good little motor started up as easily as if it were a calm dry day. It took us a long while to get home, through the choppy sea and the rising wind. I gave Lou my shorts, because I was in a floppy T-shirt long enough to cover my butt. We were both cold, though, and the light was beginning to fade by the time we got back to our jetty. The waves were slopping up over it, and banging the moored boats against the edge; I'd never seen the water come that far up, and it wasn't near high tide yet.

I didn't know how Lou had lost his clothes, I didn't know how he had come back to his own self out of the Green Man, and he couldn't tell me, of course. I don't think I was even thinking about it. There was nothing in my head but getting back home.

"Thank God!" Grand said as we came in the door, and Grammie ran to hug us. She was crying. Grand was holding life preservers and a bag of gear, and Will was with him; they'd been on their way to come out looking for us. The weather forecast that day had promised rain, but suddenly it had turned much worse. A freak storm from the Atlantic had changed its course without any warning or reason, and was heading straight for our islands, and as it picked up moisture from the ocean it was turning into a hurricane.

Grammie wrapped Lou and me in big dry towels and made us drink hot lemon and water with a little rum in it. Will gave us a hug because he was so relieved to see us, and then he and Grand went out to bring the boats up on land. The wind was picking up, rattling the windows.

"I reckon we'll all be up at the church before midnight," Will said to Grammie.

"Sooner," Grand said.

He opened the door, and the wind whirled in and hit us all in the face. "Gettin' bad!" Will yelled, and he strode out after Grand and pushed the door shut behind him. I wanted to go too, to rescue our dinghy, but Grammie wouldn't hear of it.

"They'll put your little boat in the shed," she said. "You got things to do here."

I'd never been in a hurricane, but I knew how they worked. The storm is a great whirling circle of clouds and rain, many miles across, with winds inside it more than eighty-five miles an hour, and the circle travels across the ocean getting bigger and fiercer all the time. It can sink ships at sea, and do terrible damage when it hits land. Sometimes little tornadoes develop at its edges, vicious funnels of whirling wind and cloud that can break up a house in an instant, and kill anyone inside.

And when a hurricane hits the coast, it brings a big sea-surge with it, pushing the water up twenty feet or more higher than the highest tide. That was why Will talked about the church. Our settlement is so flat that in a big hurricane the sea would cover nearly all of it, all but the one hill on which St. Peter's Anglican Church stood. When things started getting bad, everyone was supposed to gather there, to be safe from the storm.

Grammie made us fill big plastic jugs with water, and she heated some soup and put it in two thermos flasks. We collected all the candles and flashlights we could find, and rain jackets, and stuffed four blankets and pillows into garbage bags, along with Lou's yellow boom box and an ancient little primus stove. Then she had us pick up every loose object in the house—magazines, cushions, vases, pictures from the wall—and shut them inside cupboards.

"Last hurricane was when I was a little girl," she said, "and I remember. It took our roof off, and everything that wasn't tied down blew right away."

We heard thumping sounds from outside; Grand had come back and was closing the big wooden storm shutters over the windows. The wind was beginning to whine and moan in the roof. He came indoors, wet from the rain and the sea, and within a few minutes all the lights went out.

Lou started to make his nervous gasping sounds, Lou who had been so silent and brave in the dark in the Otherworld, and I felt hastily for a little flashlight I'd shoved into my pocket, and turned it on.

"Power lines are down," Grand said. He took a deep breath. "Well, Mrs. Peel, I think we all need a good supper."

So we did. Grammie had things simmering and smelling good on the stove, which runs on bottled gas, and we suddenly realized we were all ravenous. So we ate chicken and peas and rice at the kitchen table, by candlelight, with the wind howling outside and bursts of rain spattering the shutters, and it was the last meal we ate in that room for a very long time.

When we'd finished, Grand and I put on our rain jackets and went outside. The wind was whipping at the trees now, and the air was full of leaves. Grand shone his biggest flashlight down at the jetty, and we could see the waves breaking over it, and spray leaping up. High in the sky, for a moment, the moon broke through, and we saw the dark clouds, huge, racing.

"It's time," Grand said. We packed our things into the truck and he drove slowly to the church, through the woods, up the hill. Once, he had to stop where a small tree had been blown down across the road, and it took all four of us to lift it out of the way. You could see the rain slanting down in the beams from the headlights, and feel the wind gusting against the side of the truck. Lightning flashed like a great jagged split in the sky as we came to the church, and there was a huge clap of thunder. Lou whimpered, and I held his hand. The parked cars were all clustered close together, like cows in a field in the rain.

The church was full of everyone we knew. All night, people sang and prayed, and talked, and slept. The singing was the best. It was the only thing that drowned out the roar of the wind.

Around four in the morning, curled on the floor in my blanket, I woke up into the biggest noise I'd ever heard in my life. The hurricane was directly over us, hurling broken branches and uprooted trees at the church walls, and a crowd of people were pushing against the big front doors of the church to keep them from being blown in. Grammie had Lou on her lap, snuggling close. She reached out and gave me a reassuring pat.

There was a tremendous crash outside, and the whole building shook.

"What was *that*?" I heard my voice rise to a squeak.

Grand stood up, to peer vainly out of a window. "Someone's car, I reckon. Or their roof. This wind, it picks things up and throws them round like tennis balls."

But gradually after that, the noise of the wind began to die down. The crowd at the door grew smaller, and people relaxed; they lay down, or shared hot drinks they'd brought with them.

"Oh dear me," Grand said. He shook his head.

I said, "But it's stopping! Listen!"

"When it stops that fast, only means one thing," Grand said. "We right in the eye of the hurricane. Pretty soon, that wind come back just as strong—but blowing the other way." He reached for his rain jacket and pulled it on. Other people were doing the same, all around us, and I could see the rector, Father Dunn, unbarring the tall wooden doors.

Grand reached out his hand to me. "Wrap yourself up and come outside, Trey. You too, Lou. I going show you."

Grammie said unhappily, "Not safe out there, James."

Grand smiled at her. His white hair was all curly and wild from the salt and the wind. "There's time," he said. "You want to come? Most folks don't see this in a lifetime."

"Nor want to see," said Grammie, but she did come outside, with her blanket round her shoulders like a shawl.

It was hard to recognize the land around the church. Trees stood up bare and broken, and everywhere a thick layer of leaves and branches lay on the ground. Coconut palms looked like worn-out dish brushes, their fronds all battered and torn. The cars in the carpark were scattered about every which way, some of them lying on their sides. One was upside down. The roofs were gone from two little houses near the church, and there was no sign of a bird or animal anywhere.

No wind was blowing. The trees were absolutely still,

and the sky was solid grey, sullen, ominous. The only sound came from the sea, and the sea was all around us, covering far more land than it ever did at the highest tide. And it was angry, it was furious, crashing against rocks and walls, throwing spray high into the air. It was the sea that was telling us what was going to happen next.

"This the eye," Grand said.

He bent down and picked up a paper plate, from the rubbish that the wind had scattered all around us. He folded it in half, tore out the center, and opened it up again, peeking at us through the hole in the middle. Lou laughed, for the first time in a lot of hours.

"Hold out you hand, Trey," Grand said. He was teaching again, even in the middle of a great storm. He held the paper plate flat, and brought it sideways toward my outstretched hand. "Wind blows clockwise round the hurricane, so when she hit you, she blowing right to left, see? Then the eye go over you. No wind. Then the other side hit you, and she blowing left to right. You wait—you tell *your* grandchildren about this."

The plate moved over and away from my hand, and he held it up by its edge, very lightly, between two finger-tips. It shifted just a little, toward the right. A small breeze was beginning to pick up again.

Everyone went back inside the church and barred the doors, and the wind grew and grew and began to shriek and batter us again. It was the same angry roaring storm as before, the other side of the hurricane, but this time it seemed much worse. Perhaps there was more broken stuff already lying on the ground for the furious wind to snatch up and throw about. The church shook from great crashing blows that came from who knows what. It was as if there was a huge giant out there swinging a hammer at us.

I looked at Lou, sitting on the floor between Grand and Grammie with his face pressed into Grand's shoulder, and I thought of the towering Green Man, and wondered if the hurricane was an echo of him, if the power from one world had burst through into the other. In Pangaia he had destroyed the works of humans and reclaimed the land for Nature. Here, Nature was erupting to claim land and sea for itself. Himself. Herself.

Herself seemed the most right, somehow. Maybe Nature was just another name for Gaia.

* * *

When it was all over, when we had all been in the church for most of that day and night, when the angry sea had gone back from the land to something like its normal level, we could see what the hurricane had done. The whole island was brown; there wasn't a green leaf anywhere. The wind had stripped every leaf from every bush and tree; it had snapped the taller palm trees like pencils, and left the short ones in tatters. Sand and seaweed had been blown and washed inland, so that half the soil in the fields seemed to have turned to sand.

Boats left at anchor or on moorings had been picked up and thrown bodily against rocks or land; some were sunk, or half-sunk, and others lay smashed on the shore. Three of Grand's five remaining bonefish boats, and our little dinghy, had been hauled by Will and Grand into a concrete boathouse, and they were okay. The other two boats, which had been lashed to a tree, had vanished right away, and so had most of the tree.

There wasn't a single house in our settlement that wasn't badly damaged, and some were ruined. Grand's farm was a little lake of sandy brown mud, and when we reached the house, after struggling through the fallen trees and branches blocking the road, we found that the roof of the front porch had blown off, taking with it part of the house roof and most of one wall. Just one central piece of the wall was left, sticking up like a solitary tooth. It was a place where a big mirror had been fixed to the wall between two windows, and though the windows were gone, the mirror was still there on the piece of wall. It was very weird to stand looking into the mirror, seeing your own reflection among the chaos, and seeing the open ocean on either side.

The house was full of water and broken glass, and every object inside, from the rugs to the books, was soaking wet. A lot of the furniture had been crushed by splintered roof timbers and chunks of concrete. Grammie stood there looking at it all, and I could see that her eyes were full of tears. Grand put his arm round her.

"Oh James," she said sadly. "We got to start all over again."

Grand kissed her forehead. He said, "Well, we know how."

The hurricane had done other things too, and one was terrible and one was terrific.

We heard about the good thing first. Long Pond Cay, like our settlement, had been smack in the eye of the hurricane. Because it was so flat, the sea had roared right over it, destroying everything in its path. Like every big storm in the islands, it swept away beaches in one place and built them up in others, moving thousands of tons of sand. It broke down sandstone and exposed coral, it shifted shoals and altered channels. It washed away anything that would move. And it completely wrecked everything to do with Sapphire Island Resort.

Every change that they'd tried to make to Long Pond Cay was destroyed. Dredged-out channels were filled up, built-up beaches were washed away. Concrete pilings had toppled into the sea, roads were broken up, jetties and wood-framed buildings were smashed into a mess of splintered timbers. All the boats and vehicles were swept away, and even the biggest bulldozers and cranes fell and were swallowed up by the tremendous combined force of wind, water and sand. Millions of dollars, and months of work, all vanished in the night of the hurricane.

And three people were killed: men who had been working at Sapphire Island Resort and who waited a little too long to leave as the hurricane approached. They took off in a fast powerboat, but its speed wasn't enough to save them from the growing, crashing waves, and they were all lost.

One of them was our father.

FOURTEEN

The last image I had of my daddy was a face in which anger turned to blank disbelief, though somehow I felt the anger was still there underneath, anger that he had been cheated of what he wanted. I think all his life he had done whatever he wanted. These days, I try to think of the smiling photograph instead of the angry man.

They never found the three bodies, only the wreckage of part of the cigarette boat, washed up two weeks later. My daddy had no family left on Lucaya except a few cousins, and the other two men were from Nassau, so it was in Nassau that there was a memorial service for the three of them. The Sapphire Island Frenchmen paid for it. We flew over to Nassau with Grand and Grammie, and Mam bought us both new clothes, because she said it was very important for us to be at the service.

The big church was very crowded, and I remember a hymn about *those in peril on the sea*, and a long sermon by a clergyman with a beautiful booming voice, not only about my daddy and his friends but about all people who suffer from natural disasters. The hurricane hadn't hit Nassau as badly as the out-islands, but people had been hurt there just the same.

Mr. Pierre Gasperi was at the memorial service, but Grand kept away from him.

The best thing about being in Nassau was that we spent a whole week with Mam. She said that come Christmas she would be back in Lucaya for a whole week too. It wouldn't be truthful to say that we miss my daddy; the missing was all done years ago. But it would have been better to know he was alive, even if he was long gone and far away.

The damage done by the hurricane on Lucaya was much worse in some places than in others. Long Pond Cay was the worst damaged of all. Grand said it was probably hit by a small tornado spawned inside the hurricane. The government decided that the cay was after all a very unsuitable place for development, and so they withdrew all the permissions for Sapphire Island Resort, and the developers had to go and find themselves another island somewhere else.

After that, the government did the best thing of all, and turned Long Pond Cay into part of the Bahamas National Park, in the protection of the National Trust. That meant nobody could do anything to the island, ever again. It would belong to the people of the Bahamas— and to the sea.

* * *

I went out to the porch one night before bed, when Grand was sitting out there with the only drink he ever took, a rum-and-water nightcap. We were living in the house again, though the repairs still weren't finished. Grammie was doing the ironing in the living room, and she had some soft guitar music playing on the radio; you could just hear it out here. Grand had a very peaceful expression on his face. He was sitting back looking at the sky, which was all stars tonight because the moon wasn't up yet.

"See your favorite, Trey," he said. He pointed. "The great hunter. Son of Neptune."

My eyes hadn't quite had time to get used to being in the almost-dark, but I could see the three stars of the belt, and the brighter stars beyond.

"Orion," I said.

It was a kind of ritual by now, for both Lou and me— though of course Lou couldn't say the names. But Lou wasn't there, he was in bed, so Grand could just point at the first bright star, and have me name it. Then the second, and the third.

"Rigel," I said. "Bellatrix. Betelgeuse."

Grand patted my arm, and took a sip of his drink.

I was looking up at Orion. I said, without really thinking about it, "Children of Gaia."

"Gaia?" said Grand. "Where you read about her?"

I couldn't believe what I was hearing. I looked down at his face, turned up to me in interest, the bright eyes over the grey beard.

"I don't know," I said carefully. "Uh—what is Gaia?"

"An idea people have," Grand said. He settled back, looking up at the sky again. "An idea that all life on this planet, every living thing, is part of one organism. And she regulate conditions so that life go on. That's Gaia. Big Momma. Whatever one species do to damage things, Gaia will put it right, even if it mean wiping that species out."

I said, "Including us?"

"Including us," said Grand.

"You believe it?"

"I don't know," Grand said. "I'd like to."

His eyes shifted away from me, and back to Orion.

Reckless now, I said, "What about Pangaia, Grand? What's Pangaia?"

"Never heard of it," Grand said. Then he paused, considering. "Pangaia? Sure you don't mean Pangaea? That the great big huge landmass about two hundred million years ago, the one big piece of land in the sea. After that it broke up, turned into all the continents, and the islands. Even the little Bahamas, in the end." The bright eyes looked up at me. "You been readin' some interesting stuff, Trey."

"Yeah," I said. "I been readin'."

* * *

So then, one fine day, Lou and I took out the dinghy and went out to Long Pond Cay, to see how it was coming along.

FOURTEEN

This is me, Trey, remember. I'm a writer. I'm twelve years old. This is my book, the story of what happened to Lou and me.

We went out toward Long Pond, pottering along, under a blue sky, over the chalky-blue shallows. The channels and the shoals were still changing, after the hurricane, but we were beginning to get to know them. We could see the long white beach, rebuilding itself, healing the scars. One tall ragged casuarina was waving gently, among the babies starting to grow alongside it.

Overhead, there came that high little piping call: *peeeu, peeeu . . .*

It was the osprey, coasting sideways on a current of air, curving down to cross our path. The undersides of its wonderful broad wings were turquoise-white in the light reflected from the shallow sea. It swooped low over us. You could see its cruel curved little beak, and hear its plaintive loving call.

Lou looked across at me from the bow of the boat and smiled, his teeth very white in that round little dark face.

"That our fish hawk, Trey," he said. "He telling us what happened."

His voice was soft, soft but strong, like a humming-bird wing, like spider-silk.

AUTHOR'S NOTE

Even the "real" parts of this fantasy are fictional. There is no island in the Bahamas named Lucaya; the Lucayans were the earliest inhabitants of the archipelago, now extinct. No character in my story is based on a living person, and the events are my invention.

All the same, events *like* the attempt to develop "Long Pond Cay" do happen. The Bahamians and their government have to guard their beautiful islands "jealously and zealously," in the words of the former Prime Minister, the Rt. Hon. Hubert Ingraham. And so should we all guard the environment of our whole world: the earth and air and water whose quality is constantly under threat.

Anyone who is intrigued by the Gaia hypothesis should read the two books written by its remarkable originator, James E. Lovelock: *Gaia* and *The Ages of Gaia*. Also relevant to the story are William Anderson's book *The Green Man* and David Campbell's wonderful natural history of the Bahamas, *The Ephemeral Islands*.

Turn the page for an excerpt from
Ghost Hawk by SUSAN COOPER.

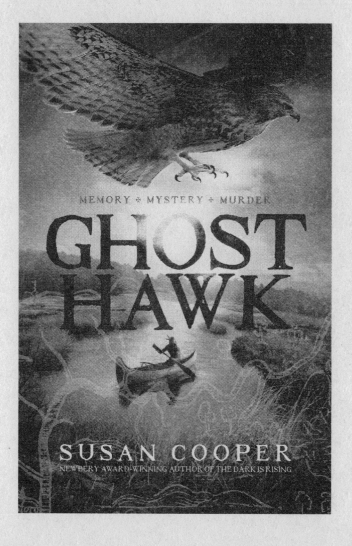

MEMORY ✦ MYSTERY ✦ MURDER

GHOST
HAWK

SUSAN COOPER

NEWBERY AWARD-WINNING AUTHOR OF THE DARK IS RISING

He had left his canoe in the river, tied to a branch of a low-growing cherry tree. Now there was green marshland ahead of him, all round the river's last slow curve. He pushed his way through waist-high grass toward one of the three high places in the marshland, where trees grew. They were islands of trees, never visited; the duck hunters went only to the marsh. He had chosen this place months ago, and now was the day to come back.

In a squawking flurry two ducks erupted ahead of him, flying low, but his bow stayed on his back; he would not hunt till later, on the way home. He reached the trees—a tangle of pin oak and cherry, sumac and hickory, juniper and birch—and threaded his way through the grabbing branches to the two rocks that marked the tree he had chosen. There it still was, beside the rocks, still the proper

shape: the small bitternut hickory tree with its twin leading stems growing in a slender V.

He gave the tree a respectful greeting, and explained
what he was about to do.

The woven birch-bark pouch was heavy round his neck.
He took out the stone blade, a long, notched rectangle of
flint with one edge chipped to a fine sharpness. This blade
had belonged to the tomahawk used by his father and his
grandfather, until its handle broke; nobody knew where it
had come from or when it was made. It was very precious
to him.

Carefully he fitted the blade into the cleft between the
tree's two slim branches, twisting them together above it.
Then, with tough strands of deer sinew from his pouch,
he bound the joined branches tightly above the stone—so
tightly that they would grow together as the years went
by, enclosing the blade.

To make a tomahawk for your son, you needed the
stone blade, and the wooden shaft, and time.

In my father's day, there was still time.

When he'd finished his binding, he thanked the small
tree, and gave it good wishes to grow straight and strong.

Then he went back across the marshland to his canoe.
On the way he shot three ducks, for the feast celebrat-
ing the arrival of the baby son who had been born early
that day.

I was that son. Because Flying Hawk was my father, the
name they were giving me was Little Hawk.

Eleven winters later, my father Flying Hawk took me to the bitternut hickory tree on the marshland. It was a longer journey than it had been for him before, because a year later our village had moved on. All the goodness of the land where it stood had been used up, by our years of growing crops on the fields, and the time had come to give the land back to the trees who would replenish it. This is the way of things.

So the crops had been harvested and packed into baskets, corn and squash and beans, and one by one the houses of elm-bark shingles and woven birch-bark matting had been taken apart. Everyone had carried the shingles and mats a long way through the forest to the new land that the men had been burning and clearing since spring, and poles had been set in the ground to make new frames for the houses.

This was home—the only one I could remember. Though

hunting or fishing would take us away in their seasons, this was now the place to which we always returned—until, once more, the time would come for us all to move on.

From here the marsh had to be reached on foot, and that took my father and me three days. But when after all our walking we came out of the woods to the open marshland, I could hear the distant breathing of the sea. And across the waving grass—fading now from green to gold—I could see the three islands my father had described to me. They were three dark hummocks of woodland, in this flat bird-haunted elbow of almost-land that the river made on its winding way to the sea.

My father headed for the smallest island, zigzagging on clumps of grass so that our moccasins would stay dry.

"We were out here on a hunt, before you were born," he said. "I saw the small bitternut then. It was already a tomahawk tree."

A tomahawk tree is a sapling with that double shoot, the two leading branches that can—with help—become one.

"If I wasn't born yet," I said, daring, "you didn't know I would be a boy. I might have been a girl."

He said quietly, "I knew."

And I saw the bitternut hickory, beside its two rocks. It was a tall tree now, twice the height of a man. The stone blade stuck out on both sides of the slender trunk, a little way below the branches; it was as deep in the wood as if it were a natural part of the tree. It had been there as long as I had been alive.

There was an odd feeling in my throat as I looked at it, like pain and happiness mixed together, and I did what my father had instructed me to do. I said to the tree, "Thank you, my brother."

My father's hand rested on my shoulder for a moment, and then he took some tobacco from the pouch at his belt and put it on the ground as a gift to the spirit of the tree. And he too thanked the hickory, and gave apologies for what we had to do.

Then he took out his own axe and cut down the tree. Because it was green wood, the trunk was tough, but before long he had trimmed it down to the first unfinished shape of the tomahawk that he and the tree had begun for me the day I was born. At home, by the time it was finished and perfect, winter would be here.

That was when I would be taken deep into the woods, blindfolded, for the three-month test of solitude that would turn me into a man. This tomahawk would be one of the very few things I could take with me, to help me stay alive.

Turn the page for an excerpt from
Victory by Susan Cooper.

FROM THE AUTHOR OF THE DARK IS RISING

SUSAN COOPER

VICTORY

TWO LIVES, TWO STRUGGLES, ONE BATTLE

On the fifth day, my uncle took me with him to the ropewalk.

Chatham Dockyard was a huge, amazing place. We walked through the streets for a long time to get there, through a warren of buildings that made me feel squashed just by looking at them. My uncle quickened his pace, and more men came hurrying all around us, all headed the same way. I began to hear a deep bell ringing, slowly at first, then gradually faster, and all the hurrying men began to run toward a high wall, thronging through tall open gates.

"The muster bell!" my uncle called to me as I ran to keep up. It meant, I found afterward, that if you wanted a full day's pay you had to be at work before that bell stopped ringing.

Ahead of us was the ropewalk, a long wooden building,

and beyond it I could see the sky full of the masts and rigging of the ships in the dockyard.

When my uncle led me in through the doors in the middle of the ropewalk I stopped dead still in astonishment. It was full of a deafening rattling noise, and the musty smell of hemp, but the most overwhelming thing was just its length. In both directions the walls, and the wooden rails that carried the rope-making machines, stretched so far that you couldn't see where they ended. It was like standing on a long, long straight road that runs to the horizon. The whole building was a quarter of a mile long, so that they could make the standard length of ropes needed for ships: one hundred fathoms. A fathom is six feet; it's the way sailors measure the depth of the ocean. I didn't know that then.

There was a huge amount I didn't know then, from having spent my whole life in the country. I learned a lot even that first day, from listening to my uncle and his friends. Everyone was expecting England to go to war with France and its ally Spain, because Napoleon Bonaparte was planning to take over all of Europe. He already had quite a lot of it. Until last year, said my uncle, we had been fighting France for years, mostly at sea. Pretty soon it would all start again, and our Royal Navy would have to fight off the navies of France and Spain and stop Bonaparte from invading the British Isles. At every shipyard in Britain, ships were being built at a frenzied rate, and since the rigging of a big battleship used *twenty-seven miles* of rope, besides heavy anchor cables and such, the ropewalks everywhere were also in a frenzy.

I watched my uncle getting ready for work, on the upper level of the ropewalk, and I was in awe of him. He was a spinner, and he was like a little king. Because I was his nephew, all the men in his team greeted me kindly, even the man in charge of them all, that they called the gaffer. I can't tell you how happy I was that day; I had never known anything like it. My uncle's apprentice, a tall, lean, young man called Will, even took time to explain the rope-making to me. He said the raw hemp came to the dockyard from Russia, in great bales like hay, and first it was soaked in whale oil to make it more supple, and then pulled through boards with metal spikes sticking up out of them, to make the fibers all lie in one direction. The men who did this were called hatchellers and they seemed to be pretty important too, but not like my uncle. Not like the spinners.

Have you ever watched anyone spinning wool? I had, on the farm; it's like magic, the way all those separate strands off the sheep's back are twisted together into one long thread. My uncle Charlie and the other spinners worked this same magic with hemp. There were four of them spinning at any one time, two at one end of the long long walk and two at the other. Each one had a bundle of hemp wrapped round his waist, its end attached to three hooks on a round frame that another man turned with a handle—and as the frame turned, the spinner walked backward, spinning those hemp fibers into yarn with his hands. It was the beginning of all rope; three strands made from that yarn would be turned into most of the rigging of a ship.

My uncle began his backward spinning walk, and the wheel frame rattled as it turned round. He glanced up and grinned at me as he backed past me, hands turning. I watched him disappear down the long walk. I wanted passionately to learn how to do what he did, one day.

Then the young man Will was upon me—"Your time for work, Samuel!"—and he set me to sweeping up loose hemp all along the ropewalk, with a broom almost as big as me. That was what I did all day, because ropewalks have to be kept clean, safe from the danger of fire. Sweep, sweep, sweep; before I was a tenth of the way down the walk I had blisters on the palms of both hands. I tried to shift the broom to different places in my hands to avoid the blisters, and kept sweeping.

Somewhere in the middle of the day we paused, for just long enough to eat the packages of bread and cheese that Aunt Joan had given us at dawn. We sat outdoors on bales of hemp, my uncle and me and the other men in his team. It was a cold day but sunny, and a release from the sweaty heat inside the ropewalk. The machines clattered on in there; when a few men were given a break, others took over, so that the work should never stop.

I listened to the men talking about the war, in wonderment at all the things taking place beyond my cottage childhood. I wished I could report it all to my schoolmaster Mr. Jenkin. The men were fiercely proud of Chatham Dockyard, and of all the ships built there. The biggest of these was HMS *Victory*, which had been built forty years ago and had just been back in the dockyard for a long refit. Every inch of her rigging had come from this ropewalk, and a lot of it spun by my uncle. Three other ships were under refit in the dry docks now. Theirs were the masts I could see beyond the end of the long ropewalk. I liked the smell of the sea, and the wild calls of the seagulls wheeling overhead.

"Keep up the sweeping, young Sam," said Will, as we went back up the narrow wooden stairs to the spinning walk. "The gaffer will take you on, I reckon. I saw his eye on you."

"Good!" said my uncle. Since the gaffer was the master of that part of the ropewalk, he did the hiring.

"I got blisters," I said proudly, and showed them.

"You'll toughen up," my uncle said. "Like this." He held out his hands to me. I hadn't noticed before, but his palms and fingers were calloused thick as leather, from years of pulling the raw hemp into a yarn.

I said, "I want to be a spinner."

They all laughed. "Very well," said my uncle's partner Henry, a grizzled old man with a big belly. "Just get yourself stronger, boy. Watch your uncle at the start of a run—that's sixty-five pounds of hemp round his waist to be carried and fingered into yarn, and he does that eighteen times a day."

And I did watch, as I swept, and marveled at how hard the work was, in this town just as in the country. But here, I could earn money, and send it somehow to my mother.

I was triple blistered, and very tired, when the workday ended and the night shift came on—the ropewalk never stopped in this time of war and shipbuilding. But the gaffer said that I could stay, so I was happy as I stumbled along with my uncle and Will through the dark streets, past glowing doorways with voices shouting and singing inside. Those were taverns, I guessed, where men got drunk. I had heard my father talk of them, with an anger that might have been envy.

It was noise from a tavern, as we turned a corner, that drowned out the sound of a brawl ahead of us in the street, and the cries of warning. "Run! Run! They'll take you! Run!" We heard the voices, but too late.

And suddenly hands seized us, and I saw my uncle twist angrily and strike out, and then fall as a man hit him with a kind of short club. I shrieked and tried to reach him, and that's all I remember. Someone must have hit me too, and I was out.